IT CAME FROM THE SWAMP

It Came from the Swamp

Edited by Joey R. Poole

Malarkey Books

ISBN: 9781088025321

Ebook available at publisher's website.

Cover design by Sarah Allen Reed.

sarahallenreed.com

Edited by Joey R. Poole.

Typeset by Alan Good.

Story titles are hand-lettered by Sarah Allen Reed.

Published 2022 by Malarkey Books.

The font used in this book is Mort Modern, a serif typeface inspired by the lettering of Mortimer Leach, and designed by Riley Cran for the Lost Type Co-op.

Losttype.com

malarkeybooks.com

Foreword

IN THE SUMMER OF 2008, car salesman Rick Dyer and since-fired police officer Matt Whitton claimed to have, frozen in a block of ice in a basement freezer, the body of a sasquatch they found while hiking in the North Georgia mountains. Teaming up with Bigfoot enthusiast/promoter Tom Biscardi, who swore to its authenticity, they sold it to a group of researchers for an undisclosed amount of money. When the ice melted, of course the cadaver turned out to be just another hoax, a rubber suit stuffed full of roadkill and slaughterhouse offal. In a series of events befitting such a backwoods caper, the pair initially tried to run off with the money, ducking out on a meeting with duped "Squatch Detective" Steve Kulls in which they'd agreed to sign a document admitting it was all a fake.

It's quite a story, full of the rash hubris that made two grown-ass men think they could get away with it and the peculiar insanity of the obsessed that allowed other grown-ass men to fall for it. It's perhaps an even better story than if it had turned out to be real. If there was a sasquatch in that cooler, scientists would have mapped its genome by now and assigned it a genus and species. It would be the stuff of sober NOVA episodes on PBS, all the mystery and possibility sucked out of something that used to exist in the murky depths of our collective imagination. This way we get the absurd humanity of the whole sordid, hilarious affair, and we still get to keep wondering if maybe, just maybe, there is something out there lurking in the shadows in the wilder parts of an increasingly paved-over world.

It's that sense of mystery and possibility that fuels the stories in this collection. Some of the creatures here, like the sasquatch if you ever find one, are flesh and blood animals. Others, like DG Bracey's Boo Hag from "Ceasing" and Edward Karshner's Appalachian golem in "Der Butzemann," are the stuff of folklore, relics of a bygone era thriving on our fascination with the unknown. Though the subject might be the cryptids themselves, the real stars here are the human beings. The predatory privilege of the men in Jaq Evans' "Flood Tide" is more monstrous than anything lurking in the shallows. Meagan Lucas' Mishipeshu, the water panther of Anishinaabe lore, is blamed for the all-too-human sins of the past.

The stories here are sometimes scary, sometimes funny, often somewhere in between. But they're also poignant, reminding us that, unlikely as we know it might be, there is always the hope that something might be out there after all. It's that possibility that keeps the grief-stricken father in Jon Doyle's "Men in the Woods" going. It's what we hope readers find in these ten tales.

—Joey R. Poole

FLOOD TIDE
JAQ EVANS

ELLA TOOK THE DOCK PATH on what her old girl scout troop leader called fox feet: toe-heel, toe-heel. By the time she passed the boat shed, evening had turned into dusk. The holly trees on either side of the path were beginning to blur into one gnarled mass, and low tide had unleashed the muck. Even with a breeze she could smell it, the soft black mud. The rot. Up at the house, the senator would pretend he hadn't noticed but it would be everywhere, that stench, until the tide came in. It would coat his walls like blood. Ella picked up her pace. The faster she grabbed enough oysters for a platter, the faster her shift would end.

Three floats drifted between the dock and the shore, or rather, the strip of mud that would disappear by dawn. Past them the estuary snaked off to the east, dark and glossy as a beetle's wing. Follow it long enough and you'd reach the Chesapeake Bay. Here, all you got was reed-choked marsh and a chorus of cicadas and peeper frogs.

Ella squatted on the dock and hauled the largest float up by its damp ropes, thumping it onto the dock with a sluice of water through the mesh. The impact released a sulfurous plume but also a tiny, translucent crab. Ella trapped it with a cupped palm, half-tempted to sneak it into late night hors d'oeuvres. The ghost crab twitched against her skin. She tossed it into the shallows and blew it a kiss as the last of the daylight fled. Something splashed near the dock, but Ella wasn't fast enough to catch more than an oval of ripples. She finished tucking oysters into the pocket of her apron and began the ungainly process of lowering the float back into the water. As she edged it off the dock, a pair of minnows slipped through the net with twin plops.

More water shifted, a slice of movement cutting in toward the sound. This time a shadow rolled beneath the surface, dark and huge and gone too fast to name.

Her grip slipped. The float hit the creek with a belly flop smack. She flinched, but no Mrs. Patterson came sweeping down the hill. Only the lap of water on mud, a thousand tiny frogs. None of them were concerned, and why should they be? Striped bass here could grow three feet in length, heavy as a toddler. But Ella stayed in her crouch and listened for another breath, just one, even though the senator and his guests were waiting on oysters and it had only been a stupid fish—

Beneath the dock, through the half-inch gaps between the boards, black water gleamed. Anything large and sly could wait down there, biding its time for a toe past the edge. A shiver tightened the skin at the back of her neck. Ella ran the whole quarter mile up to the house.

"It's all fucked. Everything. This state. This country."

Ella nodded, passing her roommate the joint. Davi took it but didn't inhale, her face blotchy and red. She'd led a protest the day before, all picket signs and chanting girls. No news teams had bothered to attend. "How can you do it?" she asked, staring at Ella. "How can you work in that house?"

"I drive there and get out of the car. It's actually pretty easy."

Ella leaned back on the couch, trying and failing to focus on the television. She'd managed to flee before the champagne was corked, but she had heard the votes come in. She'd stood there shucking oysters while Senator Walters told his dinner guests how thirty women's health clinics would have their funding stripped. Smart budget reallocation, he'd said, all modesty. Just trying to do the people right.

Davi stubbed out the joint. "I know it's a defense mechanism," she said, "I do. But if you insist on that much apathy, I insist on a lot more wine."

By the bottom of a bottle they were friends again, but Ella didn't tell her about the dock. About the shadow underneath the water, rolling, sinking down into the murk. That night Ella saw it when she closed her eyes, broader than a striped bass should be. When she slept she dreamed of floating in the creek under a bright sunny sky and beneath her, rising, something huge.

It was two days before Ella's rotation took her back to the Walters estate. Mrs. Patterson greeted her with a mop and a bucket and a fresh pair of booties, and by the time Ella finished the floors she was ready for any scent in the world that wasn't citrus cleaner. She told herself this was why she took her lunch to the dock.

That mudflat perfume filtered over the creek, but August sunshine had turned the water into a dazzling expanse of brownish gold. Still a poor substitute for the ocean, but it was harder to judge at midday.

A clang shuddered down the hill: Mrs. Patterson marking the half hour with the iron bell on the porch. Five more minutes of peace. There were bathtubs that needed scouring, cake batter to mix, student loans to repay from the diploma collecting silverfish in her closet. Ella tossed her sandwich rind past the floats and froze with her hand in the air.

Halfway on the bank directly across from her, rocking gently with the tide, was a deer. The deer was dead. When Ella first picked it out from the mess of water reeds and brambles, she thought perhaps it had slipped on the muddy shore, had broken one of its spindly legs and drowned, because its head and forelimbs were underwater. Her chest ached for such a lonely death—but no.

That wasn't right.

The empty seltzer can slipped from her hand and bounced into one of the oyster floats. Ella registered this from her peripheral vision while her eyes stayed locked on the deer. On half the deer. Because the other half wasn't underwater, it was missing. The deer ended just below the surface, torn flesh and knobby spinal cord like hauntings in the water, visible only when the sun broke through the clouds. A single strip of viscera floated in a mosaic of holly.

Mrs. Patterson rang the bell a second time. Ella jerked and caught her balance on one of the dock posts. Her empty can bobbed inside its PVC prison, almost within reach. Ella crouched unthinkingly and stretched out a hand, wrist and fingers reflected in glassy brown.

Several feet away the surface shivered.

She snatched her arm back and quickstepped to the shore. She would get the can later. With a stick.

Bull sharks had been known to swim up these estuaries. Every child raised in the tidewater knew a brother's friend's cousin who had gone creek-walking some years back and lost an arm. Whether or not it had ever actually happened in real life, the point was that it *could*.

Ella was barely off the dock when a loud splash sent her whirling to see the oyster floats rocking in a flattening series of ripples. Her heart tripped against her ribs but her feet were already carrying her back toward the water. She held a hand over her brow and squinted at the shoreline, breathing so fast the salt marsh seemed to climb inside her lungs.

The deer was gone.

The senator caught her on her way inside. He was expected back in Washington the following day, but his grandchildren were coming down to the house and would need someone to cook while Mrs. Patterson attended to a family matter out of town.

"I know you don't usually come on Thursdays," Walters said, placing a hand on her shoulder, "but we've got the room open if you want to run home and grab some of your things. I think you'll enjoy meeting the kids. Jackson's off to Johns Hopkins in the fall and if I recall correctly, you've got an interest in medicine. Maybe you can pick his brain."

Yes, Ella thought, most of her attention on the weight of his palm. *I would love to ask your eighteen-year-old grandson for his thoughts on a science I didn't study.* And Thursday was her only day off rotation, the rest of the week split between here and two other estates with live-in housekeepers who relied on suckers like Ella for the grunt work. But an extra day here meant an extra $120 and one more colored line on the thermometer-shaped poster in her room, the one labeled UNIVERSITY OF HAWAII.

Which brought her to the question of the water. While Senator Walters spoke, Ella unpacked her options.

If she told him there was a shark living under the dock, he'd suggest that maybe she ought to take Thursday off after all. He'd probably add that he understood if she needed time to adjust to the recent political news, and then he'd walk away feeling generous of spirit and Ella would have to kill herself. If she told Mrs. Patterson, the housekeeper would presume Ella had an angle and, best case scenario, ignore her.

At least no other households occupied this stretch of inlet. She could keep the stupid grandchildren out of the water for a day or two. Long enough to prove she wasn't insane.

"All right," Ella said, stepping out from under his hand. "I'll come right back after dinner."

Davi wasn't home to see Ella throw together a bag and hurry back out the door. Ella chose not to dwell on why that came as a relief.

That night she waited until the house settled down, no sound from the senator's room, and then a while longer after that. Once the moon shone hazy through a streak of midnight clouds, she crept to the kitchen and purloined a pound of hamburger.

If anyone else were recounting this story, Ella would have interrupted to ask why the hell they hadn't waited until daylight. With Mrs. Patterson gone, Walters off by dawn, and the grandkids not arriving until brunch, who would have cared if she'd slipped down to the dock before starting the quick-rise dough?

She could have said sharks were most active at dawn and dusk and she wasn't about to wake up for dawn, but the truth was embarrassing. The truth was, she couldn't sleep on a secret.

It doesn't count, Ella thought as she switched on Mrs. Patterson's best flashlight and made her way toward the trees, *if I know what I'm doing is dumb.*

The flashlight turned the hollies and loblolly pines into sharp-toothed silhouettes, and Ella hummed the only song that came to mind—a jingle for toilet paper—as she grabbed the pruning shears that leaned at this end of the dock path. It would be difficult to snip a shark the way you'd snip a rosebud, but she felt better with the cold heft of iron in her hand.

Once she entered the trees the air shifted from floral to pine-scented, although the closer to the water she got, the more sulfurous it grew. No hint of rot tonight. Perhaps the thing in the water ate its kills too quickly for them to stink.

It seemed like the path should be longer, but the dock ramp came up so fast Ella practically stubbed her toes against the edge. The tide was very present. Water glimmered an inch below the dark ring around each post that marked its high point. Ella stood at the lip of the ramp and shone her flashlight over the creek. Nothing broke the glassy surface of the oyster paddock. The floats caught Ella's light and dimmed it somehow, algae and muck and general wear stealing all the brightness until the PVC frames resembled whale bones in the dark. Ella blew a short breath and stepped onto the boards.

Plastic handles cut into her shoulder. Ella leaned the sheers against a dock post and swung the grocery bag down by her feet, taking a beat to roll her shoulder and pluck her bra strap out of the divot the bag had pressed into her skin. Then, pinning the flashlight between her teeth, she opened the package of meat.

The first chunk hit with a deep *sploosh*, ripples smoothing quickly. She counted to five and threw another chunk off to her right, toward the open creek. Cold liquid smeared her palm; she went for a third handful and the water to the right of the dock moved. Ella stilled. High in the loblollies that leaned over the water like curious old men, a pair of squirrels broke into sudden violence. Twigs and sprays of needles showered the creek.

Ella set down the meat and made a slow, unsteady sweep with her flashlight from the mouth of the oyster paddock to the shore, then in toward the floats. Nothing. Her heart beat so high and fast inside her chest that she could feel it on the back of her tongue. She bent and with trembling fingers scraped off another chunk of hamburger. The reddish lump arced over the oyster floats and down toward the water, where something reached up and caught it.

The whole thing took less than a second but it played through Ella's mind in fragments: black water, jagged shadows, falling meat. Slick gray flesh, a cartilaginous snap of fingers or claws. Ripples closing over the place where arm and meat had been.

Ella sat down hard beside the meat. Her grip on the flashlight slipped; Ella scrambled for it with both hands, and as the light jounced across the water she almost missed the V of movement coming directly toward her. *Get up*, she told herself. *Get off the dock.* But her legs wouldn't curl, her body disobeying her because it was impossible. What she'd seen could not exist. And what could not exist could not set the floats rocking in its low wake, could not slap its dripping hands onto the dock and hoist itself up to stare at Ella with two small, black eyes.

It was like a woman and not like a woman.

The idea was there, harsh in the glare of Ella's flashlight. The eyes fixed on her sat four inches or so above its head, supported by thin, glistening stalks. Two more were visible near the top of its skull, deep-set and lidless. Below those, though, was a reptilian nose and a narrow slash of mouth, and its collarbone smoothed into faint curves that might, from a distance, look like breasts. Skin like slate veined with quartz, pocked with scars on its cheeks and the insides of its forearms. Those led to long hands with four fingers each, their tips coated in knobby pinkish armor. They would skitter, those claws, like sharp-legged spiders on the dock as the thing in the water scrabbled up.

But it didn't. Scrabble. Only held itself there like a girl in a swimming pool, elbows nearly double-jointed but not quite, wheezing faintly over the cicadas. Ella had the surreal thought that it was *studying* her, examining the bones of her face that must look just as distorted to it as its facial structure did to her. Or maybe it was trying to decide the most efficient place to slash for the least amount of struggle as it yanked her into the black.

Slowly enough that Ella could feel every twitching gear of muscle wrapped around her elbow, she extended her arm one fraction at a time until her fingers grazed cold meat. The thing from the water watched her, motionless, as Ella hooked her pinkie around the damp plastic casing. Carefully she pushed the meat toward the gap between the creature's splayed hands.

It tilted its head. Then in a flash of claws, it swiped the package and flipped toward the open water. Ella caught the impression of a tail, maybe four feet long, eel-like and muscular, as warm air slapped her with the scent of mud and salt and something fresh for once, like market salmon. Cold water from the splash dotted Ella's leggings, soaking through in small but growing patches. Ella barely felt the chill.

"Holy fuck," she said. The pruning shears, unbalanced by the creature's exit, clattered onto the dock. Ella stared at them blankly, having forgotten she'd brought the tool down at all.

She must have managed a few hours of sleep, because she felt completely alert as she brushed her teeth before heading downstairs to the kitchen. Mrs. Patterson had left detailed instructions for brunch, tea, and a hamburger dinner around which Ella would improvise. For once she was grateful for the lack of faith. Ella carried out each task as though controlling someone else, a doppelgänger ready to cook and clean with no need for complex thought.

A car pulled up at ten. Jackson, tall and blond and, according to the photographs she'd dusted last week, recently freed from the Herbst that had mostly fixed his overbite. Younger sister Avery would arrive the following day, having been delayed by winning a dressage competition in Fairfax.

Jackson carried himself with the easygoing confidence of a man twice his age. He slid his gaze over Ella as she served blueberry-scarred pancakes, not leering exactly, but not shy. When she handed him the maple syrup Jackson took it with a smile and said, "Sit down and eat with me." He gestured to the place she'd set for Avery.

"Thank you, but I'm good." Ella wiped her palms against her thighs, trying to ignore the way he followed the movement. "Chores await."

"I'll be sure to tell my grandfather about your dedication." Jackson poured syrup in a light, controlled swirl. "Maybe if you finish up early you can join me for dinner. It's boring here alone."

With a noncommittal noise, Ella retreated to the sink and then the laundry room. There were sheets to wash and fold, mirrors to clean. Without Mrs. Patterson there to take all the lightweight but time-consuming tasks there was plenty to keep her busy. All she had to do was wait until Jackson plugged into one screen or another and then she could go to the dock.

By eleven-thirty, Ella was ready to strangle propriety. She stood by the marble kitchen island, mechanically stirring key lime juice into cheesecake batter. All morning Jackson had found reasons to engage her in trivial conversation, appearing behind her or easing past her in the halls just close enough to let her know he wasn't afraid to invade her space. An hour of this had pulled her skin tight and her heart rate up, or maybe it was the fact that she couldn't keep her attention from the windows that faced the creek.

She hadn't told anyone yet. Not Davi or her family or any of her other friends. Ella had started a dozen texts and deleted them all.

"Pancakes for breakfast, cheesecake for dessert. You're lucky Avery's not here. Way too many calories." Jackson leaned against the bar counter, a peach in his hand. Ella smiled tightly and focused on the smell of sugar and lime.

"Mrs. Patterson left the recipes," she said to her bowl. "I'm just following orders."

"Isn't that what the Nazis said?" When Ella didn't respond Jackson took a bite of peach and said through wet teeth, wet lips, "Smells great, though."

Ella bit her tongue hard as Jackson strolled away.

When she finally got out, the humidity had congealed until she could have tripped and fallen and the air itself might have caught her. The walk down to the dock was enough to start a slow throbbing ache behind her temples. Ella sat near the floats with her legs folded beneath her, watching the currents glint. Several fish jumped out toward the center of the creek. An osprey wheeled high before each dive. No dark shadows cut toward the dock. No dead animals on the shoreline.

Perhaps it had migrated back out toward the Atlantic. July and August were thunderstorm months; this year high winds had blown trees onto nearby power lines twice. Maybe a storm had blown the creature in too and it had made its way up the creek until it hit these tidal flats where reeds grew thick as fur. Hunting would be easy, if you didn't mind the muck. Bull sharks liked murky shallows.

Maybe mermaids did too.

Please, she thought. *Be here still.*

Part of it was the thrill of discovery, the idea of how life might look for the person who found the world's first cryptid. Hawaii and graduate school and tenure unfurling like one glorious manta ray about to soar. And the other part...

Footsteps on the path. Crunching holly leaves, the creak of the boat shed door. Ella stood, gave the water one last scan, and headed off the dock in time to meet Jackson with an inner tube under one arm and a beer in his free hand. He blocked her at the start of the path, standing with his legs apart and his chest kicked out like he owned the whole world. Which, around here at least, he did.

Yet when she looked at that bright yellow inner tube, Ella saw deer guts in the reeds. "I wouldn't go swimming if I were you." Her voice sounded a little monotonous, but thankfully didn't shake. "Tons of jellyfish."

"Oh yeah?" Jackson craned his neck to look past her. "That sucks. It's hot as balls out here."

"That's why we keep the house at 72."

"What's the point of a lake house if you can't get in the lake? Or, you know. Creek." He did a lazy up-and-down from her mouth to her thighs and back, pausing briefly where sweat tickled Ella's clavicle. "Come in with me. I won't tell if you won't."

"No thanks."

"Come on. It's just a swim. Don't tell me you don't have a bathing suit here."

Ella's heart beat too quickly. She could sense the blood whirling through her arteries, pulsing in her temples, a growing vertigo. Like being at the very top of a roller coaster just before you see the long way down.

"Seriously. Something's eating the fish."

Jackson looked amused. "Which is it, jellyfish or sea monster?" He took a swig of beer and smirked as though he were the twenty-four-year-old and she were the teenager coming onto him, and something inside Ella cracked.

"Fine," she said. "Your funeral."

Ella rode a strange high all the way to the house, a feeling that teetered between power and panic. But as she broke with the path near the manicured gardens, that balance tipped into dread—the queasy sense of realizing, too late, you've gotten a very important question wrong.

And she'd forgotten about the seltzer can, which Jackson would definitely notice and remember. Unless he was about to be eaten. "Fuck," Ella muttered, and ran.

He was out in the middle of the creek by the time she hit the dock. "Hey!" She flapped her arms above her head. The tan oval of Jackson's face tilted toward her, half his blond head darkened by the water. The inner tube held him up like an offering. "You should come in! The—the neighbor's here and he wants to talk to someone in charge!"

"What?" Jackson shouted, voice echoing faintly across the wide expanse of water. "Can't hear you!" He kicked a foot to spin himself in a leeward arc.

Ella turned to the motorboat that hung from one side of the dock, suspended by a mechanized winch and pulley. She punched the red button marked DOWN just as Jackson went under.

If he shouted, Ella couldn't hear. The winch screamed in his place as Jackson struggled to climb atop the inner tube, but it was plastic, not even freshly inflated, and every time he got one limb up a different piece of his body dipped out of sight. Before the boat touched water, the senator's grandson made like a folding jackknife.

Birds twittered over the undulating hum of insects. Out in the middle of the creek, hot air shimmered like a mirage while the inner tube spun in a lazy circle. It was half-tide. The deepest point would only have been four or five feet before the creek gave way to mud. Whatever the mermaid had done had happened right below the surface, inches from the sun.

The boat rocked against the dock with a quiet thump.

Ella wanted to run back up to the house and busy her hands making cucumber sandwiches with their crusts sliced off.

Instead she knelt and placed her palms flat on the wood, inching forward until she could peer over the edge.

At first there was only brown water and dock poles distorted by refraction. Then ten blurry fingers crept up the underside of the motorboat, found a grip on a line of rivets, and pulled the mermaid into view. The creature curled itself against the belly of the boat like a leech, tail mostly hidden but face visible through the foot of water the sun could penetrate. Its stalk eyes watched Ella. Another pair looked backward from the tops of its shoulders. There was no sign of Jackson.

"Where did you *put* him?" she asked. The mermaid pushed off the boat and vanished in a swirl of mud.

Ella reached up and pressed the button to raise the boat, then closed her eyes so she wouldn't have to watch the progress of Jackson's inner tube toward the far end of the creek. The rumble of the winch vibrated through the dock, soothing and distracting, but when the cables squealed to a halt, she nearly threw up off the side. Her vision filled with dark spots the first time she tried to stand. Eventually she managed to stumble onto shore, leaning on the heavy rope railing of the ramp, and then to the boat shed halfway up the path. Here Ella paused to sit again, head between her knees.

Already her mind was blurring events, smudging the sight of Jackson's frantic hands with the tube spinning out, as if these memories had been drawn in charcoal. When she told, she'd have to fight this instinct, would have to force herself to recount what had happened with a scientist's specificity. When she told. When she told.

Ella smacked the back of her head against the boat shed wall. Pain didn't jar the idea loose. Instead it gripped her harder, spreading over the contours of her brain like a parasite.

What if she didn't tell?

Jackson would be dead either way. He'd gotten into the water despite her warnings. Even if Ella had dived after him, there was no way to know if she would have been able to help. Maybe she'd be in the muck now too.

The police would think she was lying at first, but eventually they'd learn the truth and Ella knew what would happen next. It would be men with guns, and nets made of steel wire, and then a tank and a lab and everything scientists did when they found something new: whatever they could without killing it, and then a little bit after. She couldn't even blame these imagined lab coats. Not wholly. If she were one of them, fighting for a spot on the bleeding edge of a science already desperate for funding, she might do the same.

But she wasn't. She was a glorified maid who knew a little about cheesecake and a lot about oysters. And she was the only one who knew what lived in this creek.

A honeysuckle vine had overtaken most of the side of the shed. Ella reached out and tugged a tendril toward her, inhaling its perfume before plucking one flower and sucking out the nectar. That burst of sweetness gave her focus where pain had not, drowning out the jumble of thoughts and images until one truth remained: Ella couldn't turn in the mermaid.

Once she understood this, the rest became simple. Off-season hunters were common here. So were other accidents. You could be the strongest swimmer in the world on the quietest day of summer and you might cramp up mid-stroke, slip and hit your head, discover an insect allergy at the worst possible time. Jackson had been young and healthy but bad things happened to young, healthy people every day. Maybe sometimes they even deserved it.

Part of Ella knew, even as she dialed the police with her heart in her throat and real tears in her eyes, that shock was allowing her to give herself an excuse. Jackson had been more than eyes on her chest, more than all the little comments and insinuations.

But there were so many boys like him, and now there was one less.

The night before Mrs. Patterson reopened the house, Davi made tea despite the heat. "You don't have to go back, you know." She handed Ella a mug that smelled more like bourbon and joined her on the couch, tucking her feet beneath her. "Sudden tragedy is a good enough reason to quit."

"Those other kids drowned last summer." The mug was painfully hot, but Ella didn't put it down. "It happens. Life goes on."

"Is that what you want?" Davi asked, and Ella couldn't breathe. "More of this?"

Silence for a moment. Ella tried the tea, burning her tongue, her throat. It gave her a reason to sound raw. "If I quit, they'll think I did something."

She tried to twist it into a joke. Something must have rung false because Davi set her own mug on the floor, shifting to face Ella head-on. They sat for another beat as Davi searched for words.

"If you *had* done something," she said slowly, "I would be sure you had a good reason for it. I would believe that you were...acting with cause. Just so you know."

Ella inhaled too deeply, filling her nose with the sharp burn of alcohol, and blinked away a sudden sting. "I didn't kill anyone."

"I never said you did."

"And—" She needed to stop, she needed to put down this drink and leave the living room before she ruined everything. "He didn't hurt me." Davi opened her mouth, but Ella wasn't finished. Couldn't stop herself. "I don't know if he would've tried. I don't know."

She thought of the look on Jackson's face when she'd left him at the boat house. The way he'd passed too close to her again and again, always with a smile.

Davi nodded slowly. She leaned over for her mug and held it up. "To things we know, and things we'll never have to find out."

Ella clinked her cup and drank. The next morning, she was on the road to the Walters estate by dawn.

On the radio, pundits were discussing the sympathy vote. A press conference soundbite from the day after the accident captured the senator with his old Southern boy accent on full display:

"I love my children and my grandchildren more than I can say, and today more than ever I find myself wishing I had done more to make that clear to them. And to all of you. Our babies are what matter, protecting them. Keeping them safe so they can grow and thrive in this great country. That's a promise I've always stood behind, and it's one my choices in the Senate reflect. If we don't do right by our convictions, how can we look ourselves in the eye?"

There his voice cracked in a slight but perfectly timed show of vulnerability. Ella turned off the radio and rolled down her window, pressing the gas until hot grassy air smacked her cheek like an open palm.

That day her chores happened without her. Her body was there but—like the day Jackson died—the thing that drove it was absent. The police had found neither corpse nor monster when they dredged the estuary, but all week Ella had been afraid to think too hard about whether or not the mermaid had stayed. Now her skin itched with eagerness to go down to the water and wait.

Unfortunately, from the minute she set foot on the grounds, Mrs. Patterson watched her as if Ella might conjure up the second grandchild to lose. Ella did sympathize, distantly; it must have been difficult to know that the one day she'd left this house unattended in who knew how long, a boy had died.

Senator Walters arrived at five o'clock. He watched Ella too. Unlike Mrs. Patterson's eyes, which pricked briefly like two hot pins whenever they were in the same room, the senator's gaze was a cool hand on the back of Ella's neck. He trailed her from the living room to the study as she dusted his bookshelves and cleaned beneath each picture frame containing Jackson's grinning face. Over time the house shrank in around them until Ella felt as though she and Walters and Mrs. Patterson were dolls knocking around a child's toy, never far enough apart.

And as more sunlight sloughed off the day, the senator continued to drink.

Ella's chores were finished by seven, when ordinarily Walters would sit down to dinner and she would head back home. Mrs. Patterson hovered as Ella gathered up her bag, her real shoes. Walters sat alone at the dining room table, a tumbler of amber liquid held loosely in one hand, and followed Ella with his eyes from the kitchen to the door.

She drove her car to the end of the driveway, which was a quarter mile long and flanked by pines instead of neighbors. Ella turned right and right again, this time into an unused gravel lane that led to one of the cabins whose original occupants could no longer afford the property tax. She waited in her car for the sun to finish melting out of sight.

There was no plan. Not really. Only a feeling, *the* feeling, the one Ella shied away from naming but which had kept her from talking to Davi and had placed her on that dock more than once. She had to go back, had to make sure it was gone. Or that it wasn't.

Ella crept back down the driveway in the dark, grateful for the lack of clouds. She looped a semicircle through the woods to avoid the automatic lights and broke onto the path past the boat shed, her footsteps muffled by holly.

Only once she was on the dock ramp did she notice the can resting at the top: Jackson's beer. He must have left it before getting in the tube. Ella crouched and reached out a hand, reverting at the last instant. She hadn't even seen this the day he died.

"I asked for it back when the police finished with it. Couldn't bring myself to throw it out. Does that seem crazy to you?" Ella straightened so fast she nearly fell. Senator Walters stood at the far end of the dock, masked by the shadows of the trees. "I suppose you never know," he said, coming closer. "Maybe he'll come back for it."

Whimsical words but his tone stayed flat. The only hint of all that whiskey was the way he moved, every step a careful choice to roll his body forward. Ella stood by the boat winch, torn between sprinting back up the hill and waiting to see what he might do.

"You were here." Walters stopped beside the oyster floats and braced himself on a post. "Just you." She could see his mouth now, the quiver to it. "He's a good-looking boy, Jackson. Was."

Her heart dropped. Ella swallowed. "I told you everything I know."

"Did you?" He swayed a bit, caught himself again on the post. "I know how boys and girls think, you know. I may be old now but I wasn't always."

"Let's go back up," she said. "I can make you some tea." Though there were still five feet between them, she extended a stabilizing hand. Maybe he'd remember the kindness instead of wondering what the hell she'd been doing out here.

"Did you let him touch you?"

Ella froze. And then the senator shoved off the post and lurched forward. He closed the distance too fast for her to avoid, grabbing her above the elbow. His breath stank of something sour below the whiskey spice.

"You did. I can see it," and she was struggling but he snatched at her arms until they were pinned between them, her wrists below her chin. "Oh, you girls, you stand in front of God and country and do such horrible things. Call it a right. Is that why you hurt him? You were sending me a message?"

She couldn't speak. His words flowed into one another, thoughts too quick to follow, and he was so much taller than her, older but *strong*.

Over his shoulders, in the open water, a splash broke her panic.

"Or maybe you were ashamed," Walters said, his fingers tight on her wrists but a desperate sadness leaking into his eyes. "Women do that. Change their minds later. Ruin lives. You don't *think*, you don't want to be responsible for your choices. Someone has to do it. Someone has to take responsibility."

Each breath pulled mud inside her, deep layers of it coating her lungs. Her wrists burned in his grip. In the black water past Walters' shoulders, a patch of deeper darkness shifted like muscle under skin— and with it came understanding. The idea she'd been too scared to touch now coiled around her chest and squeezed.

"You're right," Ella said, relaxing her hands as her heart rabbited faster. The senator swayed. "Someone does."

Walters wavered again. Before her intelligent mind could catch up, Ella planted the balls of her feet, a fox-walk in waiting, and pushed.

They plunged off the dock together, but the water broke Walters' grip. Ella kicked her legs hard, rocketing backward; if the tide had been a few inches higher she would have slammed her head into the dock but instead she slipped beneath. Boards cut off the moonlight, slimy reeds twining around her calves. Three feet away the senator flailed as a dark, fleshy coil broke the surface, and then Walters jerked down. He came up once and sputtered wetly. Reached for her with one arm. Ella kicked herself further underneath the dock as water warmed against her lips, and soon the ripples stilled where Senator Walters had been.

An unnatural current swept against Ella's thighs—something large and fast swimming near. When it passed her Ella reached for the mossy underside of the dock and pulled herself, board by board, to the edge. She hoisted herself up like the mermaid had done. The rich, sulfuric stench of the creek hung all around her, cold mud clinging to the hairs on her arms. Before Ella could lever herself onto the dock, a splash announced the mermaid as it braced itself on the other side, claw tips clicking on the wood. Its face dripped red. A smaller pool stained the wood between Ella's trembling hands.

"Thank you." Blood and silt on her tongue. That fatty fresh odor cutting through the marsh. "But you have to leave now." Ella's arms began to quiver. "So many more people will come this time. They'll find you." If she didn't pull herself out this instant she was going back into the dark. The mermaid didn't move as Ella clambered onto the dock, then crouched so close she could have touched its clammy cheek. "I'm going too, as soon as it's safe. Out west. There's another ocean there."

The mermaid curled its upper lip over needle-thin teeth and hissed. Ella leaped to her feet, and despite the way her heart was pounding—or maybe because of it—she bared her teeth in a matching snarl. The mermaid hissed again, a stuttering rhythm, like speech. Like laughter. Then it shoved off the dock in a backward arc, tail slicing through the cooling night, and was gone.

The next morning, Ella arrived on schedule to a parade of red and blue. She sat in the parking lot, both hands on the wheel, and tried to keep herself from shivering. Mrs. Patterson drifted to her window. Her face was ashen, her voice faint. "Go on home. We won't need you today."

"Who's that?" called a man in a sweaty white shirt with a gun holstered below his arm. He started across the gravel lot, but Mrs. Patterson waved him off with a trace of her old imperiousness.

"No one. Just the day maid." She pursed her lips as though about to say more, then turned decisively away from the car and strode a few steps toward the house before slowing, stopping, by the roses. There Mrs. Patterson stayed.

One of the uniformed police waved Ella toward the turnabout. Heart pounding everywhere but her bloodless fingertips, she rumbled back up the long driveway and paused at the intersection. The road ahead was clear of anything but holly leaves and sun. Ella clamped her fingers on the wheel, wriggled her chilly toes inside her shoes, and drove.

Author's note:

I wrote the first draft of "Flood Tide" in 2018. It's both depressing and unsurprising to see it published in the wake of another wave of attacks on abortion rights in the United States. This is a story about what it means to have—and take—power; it's also a story about a place I love, where the shoreline changes with every storm, and the storms are getting worse. But mostly it's a story about getting fed up and doing something about it, which I hope we will all keep doing when and how we can. (Maybe without the murder.)

MEN IN THE WOODS

JON DOYLE

ASK A MAN IF THE SASQUATCH exists and he'll tell you no. If you're dull enough to ask him if they exist in the UK, he'll laugh in your face. I'm too old to worry about all that, and if it bothered Martin he never told me.

The afternoon was humid, the air so thick with pollen and dust that you could taste it on your tongue. We were out on reconnaissance, looking for sign. Footprints, hairs, scat. Anything along those lines. We didn't expect to see Bigfoot himself because sasquatch are supposedly nocturnal animals. They only come out at night.

"Anything?" Martin asked as I caught up.

I shook my head and spat on the ground. The flask of Vimto I carried was too strong and brought phlegm to my throat. I hawked it up and spat again. "We should make our way over the rise there and down into the gulley. Then circle back to where we started."

We spoke of the landscape as if we knew the first thing about landscapes. We discussed footpaths and game trails. Bluffs and creeks and gorges. Choke points where deer might congregate.

Martin's arms were sweaty and tanned and speckled with dead gnats that he'd slapped into his skin while walking. The tattoos on his forearms looked like they were sliding out of shape. A man of night shifts, Martin was nocturnal too. He wasn't used to trekking in this heat. But it was Ben's anniversary, and he always took the time off, even without me asking.

When I was a kid, maybe seven or eight, my Dad took me into the hills for what he called a day excursion. We loaded up our rucksacks with chocolate bars and weak squash and these waterproof ponchos he'd bought in the gift shop of a country park. Leaving the car, we set out with a strong yet unclear purpose, Dad with his hairy arms and battered Ordnance Survey map, me with an innocent boyhood interest in the Vietnam War. We squinted into the sun and threw stone grenades into bushes just in case. When we paused to consult the map, Dad traced his fingers over the surface and described what each part meant. He cited distances in yards and miles, made suggestions related to our course. I nodded and called yessir, enjoying his close attention, his steady breathing, the sound of the paper beneath his dry hands.

When I first realized I needed to piss, I didn't say anything. I had this thing about peeing in public, toilet or not. We kept walking, and of course, I kept needing to piss. I tried to take my mind off it. Sing songs in my head. Count the birds in the sky. But when you need to piss, you need to piss. It's more or less as simple as that.

"I need a wee," I said eventually, voice like a strangled gnat.

"Roger that," Dad replied, not breaking stride.

We kept walking. It was hard to stand up straight. I imagined my bladder popping, whizzing around like an untied balloon.

"Where should I go?" I asked.

He motioned to the treeline with his chin.

I felt my lip tremble and my father stopped walking. He crouched and put an arm on my shoulder. "Private," he said in an American voice. "The latrines are ten miles east. Marines piss in the field."

It was true. Where else would they piss? I took a deep breath and saluted, turning to march into the forest. For a moment I feared I wouldn't make it, that I'd pee my pants at the final moment, so once I was three trees deep, I got myself out and relaxed.

I remember the pure relief. A sound like leaves on a bonfire, rain on a roof. The baked smell of the earth and the weird ear-shaped growths on the ground. It was cooler under the canopy, and I savoured the aftermath before reaching for my zipper. Then things slowed down. As my fingers groped for the cool metal pull, I saw something moving. Something in the woods. A huge, hairy man, forty yards back.

He moved with languid gait, arms swinging slow like pendulums. I watched for what seemed like forever, but in reality, forever was just the time between me grabbing my zipper and pulling it up in such a way so as to snag the loose skin of my scrotum. The scene slowed further. I fell between seconds. The thing cast a look over its shoulder and met my eye.

I howled. I'd drawn blood. When Dad reached me, he got on his knees to work me free, keeping one palm cupped beneath as though ready to catch the yolk from a cracked egg. He carried me back down the trail, saying it's okay, it's okay. I said nothing at all.

At home, my mother made me sit on a bag of frozen peas. I didn't tell anyone about what I'd seen, not then or the next day or the day after that. Because to talk about the creature would have been to talk about my balls.

After Ben died, Maggie set up a charity. The Benjamin Merrick Foundation. She went around local schools and libraries raising awareness of the consequences of riding a bicycle without a helmet. Maggie and her van-load of watermelons, dropping them from various heights to demonstrate the destructive force of physics. At the end of each talk, she handed out lollipops with pink bubble gum in the middle.

Late one night, when Ben was in hospital, he asked me a question. We sat in the near-dark, legs crossed and arms folded, waiting for the worst to happen. He gestured me to the side of the bed and said "Dad? How do stories end?"

I didn't know which story he meant, let alone how it ended. I brushed the hair from his forehead and placed my palm there. I told him to shush, that everything would be all right.

Martin woke me banging pans. They say Bigfoot liked the smell of bacon, so we fried ten rashers on the camping stove. We warmed beans and sausage too, and had bread to mop up the juices, filling our bellies before we laced up our boots and headed out into the dusky evening.

The first thing you do on a night investigation is stay quiet. You load up with gear and creep through the woods. You resist the urge to talk, to check your phone. You swallow coughs and sneezes. You wait and watch.

I had a new toy. A handheld FLIR device mounted on a pistol grip. It could spot a heat signature from a hundred yards with <0.10°C thermal sensitivity. We'd gone halves, Martin and I, paying too much but not caring. We had the spare cash ever since Martin got his banning order. I hadn't renewed my season ticket in a show of support, and in truth I hadn't been enjoying football much in any case. Now kids line the concourse an hour before kick-off, throwing beer in the air like crazy people, and the stewards collar you for so much as clapping a goal.

Martin told people he got banned for putting a paving slab over someone's head in Europe, though in reality he got caught pulling a finger across his throat over the divide at West Ham. I stayed in the ground that day and we lost 1-0. It felt like a sign.

I looked for anything red or yellow or white. Anything hotter than the trees. Martin followed with a parabolic microphone, listening for grunts or calls. Sasquatch communicate that way, which was something we learned online. YouTube, internet forums, we followed it all. Rooting for our favorite researchers. Hoping they might catch a break.

The first-person view of the forest. The sound of footfall on loose brush. The heavy breathing of the host. I loved it all. Martin said I watched so many of these videos I sometimes talked like a Yank. Like I was slowly becoming one of them.

Through the FLIR monitor the woods were cast in a psychedelic scale, purple and orange and white. I got to use it first. Martin came to Bigfoot through television, watching Unsolved Mysteries and Beyond Belief, Arthur C. Clarke's Mysterious World on ITV. The Patterson-Gimlin tape was no more or less prevalent in his mind than the Zapruder footage or Arizona's Phoenix Lights. It was personal for me.

The second thing you do on a night investigation is a series of wood knocks. The clue is in the name. Get a stick, hit a tree, hope the sasquatch knocks back.

They do this amongst themselves, the experts claim. A communication thing. Martin brought an old rounders bat he found in his mother's shed. She'd been something of a hoarder, Martin's mother. Piles of cereal boxes and TV Guide magazines. I found a decent-looking oak, at least what I thought was an oak, and signaled for Martin to turn off the parabolic.

"Should I have the FLIR—"

"Shhh!" I said, raising a finger to my lips. I waited for silence before shaping up, poised to strike, counting down in whispers.

Three...two...one...

Thump.

The noise was gone as soon as it had appeared, sucked out into the black night. We held our breaths and listened. Nothing. I shook my head and raised the bat to—

Thump.

We stopped. I wide-eyed ogled at Martin and he wide-eyed ogled back. "Do it again," he hissed.

I blinked hard to clear my head and wound up slugger style, two-handed like Babe fucking Ruth.

Thump.

We held our breath. We waited.

Thump.

"It's getting closer," Martin said. "Keep knocking."

Thump.

One reply could be a coincidence, two was uncanny. A third would seal the—

Thump.

Martin cocked his head like a dog. "It's moving off," he said simply, staring out into the trees.

I picked up the FLIR and scanned the treeline but there was nothing, not even a lingering ghost of heat.

We didn't last long after Ben died. Maggie wanted to keep his room just as it was and it seemed like my duty to disagree. We argued a bit, but mostly sat in silence. It felt like we were no longer connected, like when we first met and either of us could have just left the room and never come back. There were no ties anymore, no consequences. One day I walked out of the front door and sat in the car all night. I came in the next morning and poured Crunchy Nut Cornflakes into a bowl and she said nothing at all.

Then came the Bigfoot thing. I began to find that I preferred to be watching those videos to watching TV. I preferred watching them to sleeping in my bed. I didn't want Maggie to ask what I was doing. I couldn't explain it to myself. But she didn't ask, not once.

We separated a while later. Maggie set up the Foundation, I tried to feign interest. Sometimes she'd call and we'd talk about nothing in particular until the conversation turned to her school visits. She'd remember the names of the kids, the teachers, how they had reacted and what they had said. She'd tell me about the kids that reminded her of Ben, describing the way they sat or said their S's. She'd speak conspiratorially about other grieving mothers, as though their lack of Trusts and Funds suggested some lack of depth within their grief.

People are different, I told her, they grieve in different ways, and her laugh crackled down the phone.

If you want to escalate possible contact, you move on to whistles and whoops.

It's a lot harder to whoop like a squatch than knock like one. Martin's vocal cords had been battered by Benson and Hedges, and neither of us could whistle, so the honour fell to me. We pushed further into the forest and I tried to mimic the noises I'd heard online. We walked a hundred yards and tried again. I issued a sequence of three whoops and we waited. We walked some more and whooped some more and walked again.

The last thing you do on a night investigation is a call. Which is to say, yelling at the top of your lungs in the hope a Bigfoot yells back. It's make or break, to be used only in complete desperation. Either you trick the creature into replying, or you alert every sasquatch in the area to your status as a human being. Do that and they melt into the landscape quicker than a witch in water. Your investigation is done.

The process is complicated by the fact that there are a variety of different vocalizations attributed to Bigfoot. Choose wrong then you might as well pack your bags and haul ass home. There are high-pitched screams that sound like a woman getting murdered, and low guttural grunts like a gorilla might do. There's even a conversational kind, a proto-language called Samurai chatter, gabbling and gibbering through the trees.

Our call of choice was long and loud, a full-throated yell known in the profession as the Ohio Howl. One last Hail Mary, screamed into the dark.

We decided to do it together, climbing onto a small crest in the hope that the sound would carry down the valley. This time Martin counted on his hands—three, two, one—and we let loose.

Upon reaching camp, we built a fire and set to drinking. I got some kindling lit and Martin dragged in some bigger branches. Soon we had a decent one going. Fires were banned in the summertime but there was no substitute for a good drink around a real blaze.

"I was thinking," Martin said.

We'd settled into our camping chairs, cheap things we'd found in Lidl that probably shouldn't have been so near the flames.

"Bigfoot are from America yeah?"

"Yeah."

"Then how did they get across the Atlantic?"

I took a long draw from my beer. He had a point.

"It's just I watched a programme once about this zoo and it said on there that gorillas can't swim. They put a moat around their enclosure to stop them escaping."

I nodded and took another long sip. The branches we'd chosen must have been full of sap because the fire was starting to spit.

"If gorillas can't swim, do you reckon sasquatch can?"

I nodded slowly, swirling Stella around my gums. "What about ice ages?" I asked. "What about continental drift?"

Martin didn't reply for a long while. Eventually, he shifted in his chair and frowned. "Didn't think of that," he said.

The spitting got worse. Soon the flames were glowing a blueish green. We watched with great interest. The hiss reached a crescendo, followed by an almighty thud, and then the fire settled back into an easy rhythm.

"Well that was weird," Martin commented.

I agreed. I'd never seen anything like it. It got you thinking about how big the world was. About the strange stuff that could happen. How much started and finished unseen? Flashes out of the ordinary. Tiny, inexplicable moments unfolding with no audience at all.

"Do you believe in aliens?" I asked Martin.

"Yeah," Martin said. "You?"

"Probably," I admitted. "Out there somewhere anyway."

There was a bird calling someplace, even at this late hour. Neither of us were bird people. "Believe in ghosts?" he asked.

"I dunno," I said. "Do you?"

"Nah."

"Well," I said. "Ben used to get up at three every morning to piss. He'd hit the same loose floorboards. You could set your watch by him. For months after he died, I'd hear the same noises."

Martin looked apologetic. "I don't know," he said. "I might believe in ghosts. I might believe in anything, really. Who knows?"

I nodded sagely and raised my beer in his direction.

"I didn't realise you'd seen spooks too," he said, draining his can. "You're like a bloody magnet for this stuff."

"I haven't," I laughed as Martin opened another tin. "I'm just saying."

"Seen anything else?"

"Just the squatch."

"Right out here?" he pointed off into the trees.

"If not here then somewhere a lot like it."

Martin belched and drank his Stella. "So...what happened then?"

"What?"

"You've never told the story. Not all the way through."

Fuck it, I thought. It's only Martin.

"I was out here with my old man. He used to take me on 'expeditions.' We'd pack bags and spend the day wandering. This one time we were on a long trek, and after a few hours I needed a piss. Like, badly. Only I was a soft kid and didn't like pissing in public, even in the toilets. So I didn't say anything. I held it. Course, it just got worse. Long story short, he convinced me that no one would see me in the trees.

I traipsed in and had the most fulfilling piss you could ever imagine."

"And what, you splashed his toes?"

"Almost," I chuckled, opening a new can. "I was standing there, basking in the afterglow, and I saw him. About forty yards ahead. Clear as day."

"And then what?"

"I just watched him."

"For how long?"

"For...I dunno."

"What about your old man? Did he see him too?"

I took another long drink and set the can at my feet. "Here's the thing. While this was going on, I was also zipping up. Only, somehow I got my angles wrong and snared my ball sack too."

Martin was pale but hungry-looking, wanting further details in spite of himself. "Like...hard?"

"Really fucking hard. Hard enough to see stars. Hard enough to draw blood."

Martin started to laugh, and I found myself laughing too. We laughed until I kicked over my beer and we laughed at that as well. We laughed at the crackling fire and our shitty tents and we laughed at Martin's seven years away from football. We laughed at Maggie's watermelons, at her lollipops. We laughed at whoops and whistles, the Ohio Howl.

"You should recreate it," Martin said suddenly

"Recreate what?"

"Your encounter."

Recreations were a staple of the Bigfoot research community. Line things up as closely as possible, get a sense of size and scale.

"Retrace your steps," Martin said. "See if it happens again."

Maybe it was the sixth can, but it made total sense. I drank the remainder of the Stella in my hand and then downed another, too full of purpose to vomit. Martin seemed to cotton on because he donated one of his cans too. I worked my way through our weekend stash like there was no tomorrow.

The desperate need to piss arrived alarmingly quickly. I stood without a word and walked into the trees. I looked for the ear fungus along the ground.

To my delight, I found some. Not the blanket of my youth, but a single, wet-looking growth. For an awful moment I thought I wouldn't be able to go with Martin nearby, but when I swallowed and unzipped, the release was automatic, instinctual, a sensation so marvelous I almost called out in joy. It got me thinking. About Martin and Maggie and me. How we were all just carrying on. About what I was doing, out in the middle of nowhere as morning broke on a Sunday. What was I looking for? I knew I'd never see him. Never hear his voice. I tell you, I'd settle for the smallest sign.

The stream died down to a trickle, the trickle to a drip. I shook a few times. Swallowed. I reached for the zipper and I did not hesitate.

My son once asked how stories end. I guess, mostly, it's kind of like this.

Author's note:

There's an episode of Animal Planet's Finding Bigfoot in which they visit the UK. The show refused the obvious scripting of its rivals in favour of enthusiastic investigation, but even the most excitable members of the team struggled to believe the infamous sasquatch could be hiding in the relative postage stamp of British woodland. They ended up at Loch Ness instead, but not before meeting men, always men, who swore they had seen something. It got me thinking. What would it be like to see the unbelievable at a time or place even the believers wouldn't buy? There's a preconception about men like that, but perhaps it's not as sad as you think. Perhaps there's something human in wanting to believe in more than there appears to be.

CEASING

D.G. BRACEY

"It just ain't the same." Boo hissed the words. "Everybody's got cameras on their phones now. Everybody's a celebrity."

"I ain't worried about phones," Skank huffed. "It's the Caterpillars and Deeres that got me pissed."

"Animals and bugs?" Boo asked.

"No." Skank blew a deep sigh out of the side of his alligator smile. "Tractors and haulers been ripping out the swamps and throwing up those cookie cutter suburbs."

The creatures sat at a cross-street café—a table full of chicken bones between them. A half-dozen glasses of melted ice made the table an obstacle course.

"There's so much to be scared of these days that nobody's scared of anything," Boo said. "With human traffickers and serial killers and pedophiles and hacker kidnappers and whatever the hell else they can come up with. We're like the last thing on their list. Hell, we're not even on the list."

They sipped their drinks, looked out at Halloween night in Charleston. Costumed ghosts and goblins roamed King Street and Calhoun. The bar-crawling Santas, soaking bourbon through dirty white beards. Their drunken elves tagged along, bells digging a shanty off their pointy hats.

"They'll come back, they always come back to the monsters," Skank said. "Myths are forever."

Boo shook her head, pulled hard on a straw full of Mai Tai, pointed out at a circle of frat boys, all different versions of vampires—Nosferatu and Dracula and goth vamps. "These idiots are the monsters now."

"The doubt...it happens to us all," Skank said. "Why are we here? What is our purpose? How does any of this matter?"

"It's not that easy. I literally live off other people's energy, their souls." Boo looked up past the retro gas-lamps, gone electric for a century now, only antique-looking shells. "These people are soulless. The fear of the dark. The endless terror of silence. The restless dread of the Gothic. The superstitions of the islanders. It's all gone. And we're dropping off like flies because of it."

"No." Skank put his whole scaly body into the denial. "There's plenty of us still around, making the night our playground."

"You know Nessie ceased, eons ago," Boo snapped.

"Well, Nessie got caught cold. The pictures, fishermen caught him on a net for Christ-sakes," Skank said. "She had to cease."

"Sassy ceased too," Boo snapped again.

Skank backhanded the air with a flip. "Sassy got sloppy too, left tracks everywhere. Hunters are still finding tracks."

"Those hunters are about all the believers we got left," Boo said. "They're the faithful that still see Jesus' face in the toast, the potato chips."

"What about Jersey?"

"Nope," Boo blurted.

"You're crazy." Skank looked away, to the bustle of the street. "The devil's still out there, prowling the pines."

"He's gone, Skank...can't you feel it?" Her red skin darkened, gave off a heat. He could see her chest rise and fall under her raincoat. He heard her heart beat heavy between her loose, skinless cleavage. He could feel the hollow, out there, the emptiness of a moth's flutter. He heard the giggled breath trapped underneath the cloudy night. He felt the nothing, the void.

"How many are left?" Now, his hand grasped his glass, loose, weak. He let a finger trace a drop of the glass's sweat.

"Not many." Boo matched the dropped mood. Her hand moved toward Skank but stalled on the table. Her pale lips turned. Her sharp teeth showing, a faint smile. "Encantado is still kicking around the Amazon, still a pervert. And there are plenty of monsters out at sea. The major mountain ranges still have a handful. Scandinavia won't let go of their creepy crawlies."

Skank nodded, gave a not-bad grin, but before Boo could let the heaviness drift, she said, "But the rest of us are few and far between."

Skank slammed a clammy fist down on the table. "We've got to do something?" he barked.

"Like what?" Boo sat back, an uninterested look in her far-away eyes.

"Let's kill some flesh-bellies." Skank showed his teeth, his tongue wild in his long mouth.

Boo twirled her long hair. The tangled black and gray strands seemed to straighten as if awoken by her touch. She said, "Won't work."

"Damn it, why not?" Skank snapped.

"They'll just blame other flesh-bellies." She snatched at a tuft of hair with her razor-sharp nails.

"We'll leave evidence that we did it." Skank leaned in. "We'll come out of the night and rip them apart and leave swamp slime, and you can steal their skin and their souls, and we'll leave them sunken and broken and skinned. They won't know for certain that it's us, but they'll know it was the unknown, the mythic."

"Won't matter." Boo didn't budge, but her hair had begun to dance on her head without so much as a stir of wind. "Don't you see...we're not even a consideration. Plus, I don't have the energy for all of that anyway."

Skank slunk back in his chair, and they sat quiet in the chaos of the café. The coming and going of the aged and the young, all stinking of life and possibility.

Skank sprang upright. "Then, let's merge and make a new monster." His eyes lit up, his spirit resilient, unable to give in. "We can raise it right, teach it to be a monster for the new millennia."

Boo shrugged. "You just want to merge."

"Well, yeah, but think about it. A new monster will give us new purpose, new reasons to live in the shadows." Skank reached across the table, his hands moving like he was sculpting the words with wild gestures. "We can watch our little monster rule the night, make new myths...it could bring us back, just by association."

Boo smiled that sad and wicked smile. "That makes us look desperate."

"We're two mythic creatures sitting in a restaurant, eating lemon-pepper wings like a couple of flesh-bellies...flesh-bellies all around us." Skank slapped the table. "We are desperate."

"Fair enough." Boo hailed the waitress with a wave to bring the check. "I got nothing else to do."

"Yeah?" Skank grinned his crocodile grin.

"Yeah," Boo said. "Let's make a monster."

They walked down the cobblestones. The pads of their bare feet smacked echoes off the mud and brick of the broken buildings downtown. The earlier rains puddled in low spots. The night seeped and roamed in shadows along the side streets and narrow alleys.

As they came to some maverick gravestones in a courtyard, Boo lingered from time to time and listened for the whispers and scratches of lonely ghosts, lost in the heavy air of the fall.

Not a peep reached out to her, not did any specters scurry away from them. There was just more nothing.

"What happened to the world?" Boo sounded like she might cry.

"Immortality has its ups and downs." Skank searched out in the shadows, waited for a mortal to come stumbling along, drunk. He wanted to scare the piss, the literal piss, out of some moronic flesh-belly. "Remember when paved roads came along, or home cameras and alarm systems, or even streetlights? They been pushing us into tighter and tighter corners for eons."

"Skank, I'm a Boo Hag, a succubus, I can move as mist and hide in a teacup."

"Fair enough." Skank eyed a locust caught in his spire, widening in a loop around the upcoming streetlight.

"You can run back to your swamp," Boo said. "I'm drenched in this world and wrung out by their apathy, their empty eyes, their numbed nerves."

"I can still get that burn from their fear, that sweet drip of adrenaline oozing down my throat, that bliss of their memories that flood before certain death." His eyes circled with the loop of the locust. His tongue lashed a whip-shot, sucked the armored bug straight down his gullet. "I don't need to live off their raze like you, I can live off one sucker a year, every other year sometimes."

They came along the Battery, saw the twenty-somethings gathered around a bench across the park. A couple climbed on a prop cannon, flirting, and passing a joint one way and a bottle of flavored vodka the other.

"Look at them, dulled beyond their beliefs. They barely have sex anymore. It's all virtual and digital and screens and more screens. It's beyond kink because everything is normal now."

They strolled along the park's edge. Massive oaks cast shadows and shielded them from most of the moonlight.

"Last summer, I took a boy in his sleep," Boo said. "He was barely past a teen, maybe 20, 21. I climbed on top of his chest, bore down my heavy cloud on his head. My essence pushed into his thoughts, heated his dreams, tried to liquefy his little soul so I could drink it up."

Boo's eyes burned green neon like the steam from a witch's brew. Her face pulsed bright red and simmered bright and crackled as the memory of her act worked on her like a rising orgasm.

"Yeah?" Skank said. "Then what?"

"He just fell deeper into sleep, his body laden with melatonin. He barely acknowledged me." Boo's body cooled and turned into the hue of cold salmon. Her eyes extinguished to coal black. "They all exist on this cocktail of Adderall and Prozac and porn and sleep aids. I was a lukewarm, damp dream to him."

Skank reached out to console her, but she pulled away.

"Give me back the terror of rigid religiosity. Give me the fight for survival. Give me the battle of good and evil. Give me interrupted night prayers so I can rip a soul clean from a body and leave them empty and moaning for God to save them."

"We're in the South, there's still plenty of God-fearing to be had."

"They've seen too much, almost all of them," Boo said. "They're faith isn't a suit of armor or a weapon anymore. It's a scarf that keeps their necks warm."

"We're all jaded, Boo," Skank said. "We just have to get back in the loop."

Boo nodded, her eyes shimmered Spanish red, a rojo, with tears—angry, sad, and bulbous tears.

"Come now, let's see what terrors we can make together." Skank slid over the wall of the Battery, down the rocks and into the harbor.

Boo followed, hovered over the rocks, straddled Skank's back and he navigated the harbor, back out to the Ashley River, to a Cypress grove. The two monsters moved without words on the muddy bank, and when Skank began to speak, Boo clamped his long trap shut.

Her hair wafted in smoking spirals. Her eyes burned again. Her raincoat slipped open, fell away, her body moved like targeted fog, surrounding Skank, and entering him, through his every pore.

He shook. He grabbed at the smoke as it poured through him. He splashed into the water, waist-high and began his death roll—The Lizardman's Death Roll, only now, he was tangled with her, and they rolled together in a roll of bliss and potential birth.

The moon pulsed above them. The fall air heaved with them, and they moaned and screeched and purred and howled and rolled feverishly in splashy delights.

Skank woke. The night had almost escaped. The haze of morning eased in. He felt the heft of the egg inside him. He knew this may change everything, or this egg might crack early and leave him with a shard bowl of green jelly and smoke. But the potential was there.

He lowered himself into the water and headed upstream, back inland, back to the still waters of the swamps, back home. In the estuary, a great blue heron perched on one leg just in the shallows, in a mess of fallen trees. Skank's body submerged, shifted, and pushed him through the water. His head, the only piece of him revealed, glided without so much as a ripple. The bird, majestic and clueless, plucked at his down.

With a surge and a snap, Skank sprang and engulfed half the bird in his mouth. A crunch of bones and a spray of bloody feathers—four bites and the broken bird slipped in gulps to his gullet. He plopped down on a felled and rotting tree trunk. The egg with its soft and veiny shell beat like a heart inside him.

He closed his eyes and searched the world for the heat of Boo, for her presence seeping into the morning fog lifting over the water, moving along the tide. He waited to hear that song all creatures sing without even knowing it, that secret emission letting the others know they're still there.

But he felt nothing. He heard nothing except the toads croaking and the water flowing, full of debris, toward the mouth of the ocean.

Author's note:

I thought it was a funny idea—two mythic creatures, old friends, out on a date on Halloween night. Everyone is drunk and costumed so it allows them to be themselves. But there is also this playful ennui, this weariness because the world is changing and leaving them behind. It riffs a bit on the rom-com My Best Friend's Wedding...like if we're still single after two centuries, we'll merge and create a new monster for this new millennium. As far as cryptid characters—I grew up with these monsters—Skank aka the Lizard Man and Boo Hag from Gullah folklore. I come from a family of storytellers. Someone always knew someone who knew someone who had been attacked by the Lizard Man or saw the Boo Hag above them when they woke up in their dark bedroom. It also helps that these cryptids are from the Carolina coast and the swamps. Wetlands make for great settings. There is so much life bustling in murky waters and creeping in the humid shadows that once you add the characters' voices, it feels like writing a muddy fugue.

THE MONSTER BENEATH
MEAGAN LUCAS

Now – Spring 2018

MINNA'S MOTHER SET THE MUG on the scarred wooden table. Minna wrapped her cold hands around it. The mug was one her mother had made, but deemed unsellable. The glaze was the exact rich cobalt of Lake Superior on a July afternoon, but smoke had gotten in the kiln, adding blots of dark gray and black, hints at the danger beneath the waves. It was Minna's favorite mug. She looked to the basket where her mother kept the Coffeemate, and a bottle of maple syrup, and then stood to grab the sugar bowl from the buffet. Her sidearm caught against the edge of the table with a clatter.

Her mother winced.

"Sorry," Minna said and stirred four heaping spoonfuls of sugar into her brew.

"Someday that's going to catch up with you," her mother said, patting her farm wife hips. "Being the sheriff is a lot more pressure. It's hard on your heart."

"I'm not really the sheriff."

"Yet," her mother said and wiped a generous smear of butter on her pulla and took a bite.

"Interim," Minna said, and then smiled and said: "For now."

Minna's phone rang. It was her deputy. "We got a body," he said in his usual soft-spoken brevity. Her heart raced.

"One sec," she said into the phone as she stood, the chair screeching across the floor. "Sorry Mama," she mouthed as she ran out the side door and across the slushy drive. "Okay, shoot," she said, every nerve in her body snapping and ready.

"Twenty-something female. Agawa Bay. Appears to have washed ashore. Puncture wounds on her leg. Perhaps an animal bite. Found about an hour ago by some local boys. We are securing the scene."

"Make sure they leave the body in position. I'm on my way." As Minna hung up and turned to open the driver's door, she was surprised to see her mother standing in the slush.

"A body?"

"Not him," Minna said. "Female."

Her mother nodded, and handed her a piece of bread wrapped in waxed paper. Minna hugged her mother, got in the truck, and then left her behind. In Northern Michigan distance was measured not in miles but time. In twenty minutes, Minna would see her first dead body as Interim Sheriff, and only her fourth in the fifteen years she'd been on the force. But every time she wondered if it was him. And every time a body disappeared into the cold dark of

Lake Superior she wondered if it was Mishipeshu taking someone else.

Then - Fall 1991

Winter was near, fog clouded the windowpanes. Minna's daddy usually put plastic over them to keep out the cold, but he hadn't yet. A draft brushed her bare knees beneath the Michigan Tech t-shirt she stole from his drawer and wore to bed every night. Minna looked out to the sky darkening behind the trees, and wished she could see the lake beyond. She imagined watching her dad coming across the water in his new blue fishing boat, named after her, running downstairs and telling her mama and pappa that he was home. She'd had this wish for a week now.

"You're supposed to be in bed, little one," Pappa said from the door. The light from the hall spilled warm around him into her darkened room. "Come now, I'll tuck you in."

Minna didn't want to sleep until Daddy came home.

"Come now, I'll tell you a story."

She turned at that, toward her grandfather, his hair sticking straight up from pulling off his toque. She got under the covers.

"When I was a little boy, almost exactly your age," he said, pulling a chair to the side of the bed, speaking low, more like a whisper.

"Tell me the one about the storm."

"Not tonight."

"Yes tonight. I want to hear a true story."

He said: "I only tell true stories. Now, your mother is going to be mad...fine, fine, settle in. When I was a wee lad, I went fishing with my pa one morning before school. Mama didn't want us to go. She didn't like the look of the sky. She thought a storm was coming. My pa thought that it was hogwash, and that women were always worried about the sky. If it was raining, they'd holler about umbrellas and boots, snow it was toques and mitts, hell, even in the sun they went on about sunscreen and dehydration. They were never happy, he said, so he ignored her.

"It was cold, even for November. Windy, misty, like God was spitting, but we bundled up because we knew we only had a few of these mornings left before the bay iced over. It was still dark as my pa dropped anchor on our favorite spot, a little cove tucked beside a cliff. When I stood to cast my line, I noticed how wild the lake was. The waves were huge, even in that protected cove. The waves were so large that the boat rocked and we rubbed against the cliff wall, scratched the gunwale all up. Pa cursed. It started to rain harder, the water was getting under my hood. I was starting to think Mama was right, but couldn't say that. Instead, I said: 'We should go back. I got to go to school.' It was so dark, we still had the lantern on, and he went to argue with me but looked at his watch first. I remember how all of the color fell out of his face. It was much later than he thought. It was dark because of the weather. Not the time.

"'Put your lifejacket on,' he said. And then tried to start the boat, but it wouldn't turn over. All I could think about was Jeffrey Smith, a boy in the grade above me. He had gone missing that summer. He and his dad had got caught out in a storm. Their boat was found days later, upside down on the rocks, but they never found Jeff or his dad. All anyone at school talked about was what it felt like to drown. If you'd be able to feel the water in your lungs, taking your breath. Or if the temperature of the water would make you numb, and you could just watch as you sunk to the bottom. Others were convinced that Mishipeshu took them, but everyone was afraid to talk of her, as if saying her name would summon her from the deep.

"I just watched the light bulb in the lantern and tried to ignore how many times my dad yanked that starter. We hit the cliff again. He made me hold an oar out to keep us off the rocks. I was trying, but I was all of seventy pounds then and that oar was heavy, and the wind and the waves—I'd never seen them like that before. I tried to hold on, but a bigger wave came, and stole my weight. I was airborne, and when I reached out so as to not end up in the water between the boat and the rocks, I dropped the oar. Then we had nothing but the two of us, two rods, a dead motor, and a lantern; and a lake that wanted to swallow us. I knew the next wave would be the last.

"I watched the swell of the dark water move toward us, charging like wild horses across a field.

"I watched the side of the boat rise in the air above my head.

"I turned to the space between the boat and the rock, the space where I should soon find my small body trapped in icy water, but there were scales there instead of water. And spikes. And eyes. Big, intelligent eyes that looked into mine as she held up the side of the boat.

"My dad had the pull start in his hand as he fell and it finally yanked hard enough to start the motor. As he drove the boat out of the cove, I tried to find her again, but I couldn't. I only got that one time. The time she saved my life."

"Do you think she saved my daddy?"

"I think she would if she could."

"And if she couldn't?"

"Then I think she took him down to her home in the very bottom of the lake and is taking very good care of him there."

"I wish you wouldn't fill her head with nonsense," said her mother from the door. "It's not like we aren't having a hard enough time without fairy tales."

"Mishipeshu is not a fairy tale," said Pappa. "I saw her and I'm not the only one."

"Minna, say night-night to Pappa. You've got school in the morning."

Minna rolled over so she could look out the window, stuck a piece of her white blond hair into her mouth. Her mom and pappa were arguing in the hallway. Her mama never liked stories about what lived below the surface of the lake. She couldn't believe in things she couldn't see, she said, and that went for God and Mishipeshu or whatever, and she didn't think either of them had her husband.

Whenever Mama talked like that Minna put her fingers in her ears and pressed her tongue against the roof of her mouth and counted the ridges.

Her daddy was Sheriff Kokkenen. Her daddy was who you went to if your dog was missing, or if you got separated from your mom at the grocery store. He rescued people from burning car wrecks and found them lost in the snowy woods. He stopped bad guys and saved the day. He would come back to her; it was just a matter of when.

Now

Lake Superior has plenty of beautiful beaches, Agawa Bay was not one of them. It wasn't a surprise that a body would wash up here, the currents were strong, and the waves seemed to beat on the land even when the rest of the lake was calm. Minna climbed over the rocks and picked her way along the stony shore to meet her deputy, Rankin, and two medics.

"No footprints but the boys' when I arrived," Rankin said by way of greeting.

They hadn't had any new snowfall in days. The woman hadn't walked or been carried in. She'd washed ashore, and Minna could tell. She was soggy. Her naked body: white, gray, and purple, verging on translucent, except for the dark puncture marks in her mangled lower leg.

Minna squatted for a closer look. "Bear?" she asked, but knowing that her guess was off, the bite wider than a bear's muzzle, more like a fish, or a big cat.

"Looks more like a sturgeon," one of the medics said. "You know they pulled an eight-footer out over in Marquette just two weeks ago. She looks like she could have been in the water for more than two weeks. Minna stood, rubbed her outer arms, and then walked over to Rankin, who was taking pictures of everything.

"No local girls missing. Send these pics to the state cops and see who she is. Get these guys to pack her up to the ME then I guess we wait our turn for news. About all we can do," she said and then nodded to the medics who slid the woman onto the backboard and carried her to their vehicle. Minna looked out to the water and shivered.

"You want me to check with the Canadians?" Rankin asked.

"That's a good idea. Jesus, I wonder what happened to her leg. The ME will have to tell us if the water killed her or not, but that leg...fuck, those wounds say that that horror happened when she was alive."

"I know what you're thinking."

"I know you do. Don't worry, I won't say it out loud. I won't tank my career before it starts. But seriously, doesn't it look like it?"

Rankin was trying to hide a small smile when Minna's stomach growled loudly.

"You headed home for dinner then?" Rankin asked.

"Nah. Chris is meeting the realtor."

"I don't know if I told you how sorry I am for your loss?"

"You did. Thanks." She turned and smiled at him. "I think I'm going to look around a bit and see if anything else has washed up."

"I'll help."

"You go home to your girls. I know they'll be missing you."

Deputy Rankin frowned the way he always did when she said something like that. Something meant to be nice but served as a reminder of her heartbreak. She looked over at him and smiled. "Go," then chuckled, "that's an order."

"You're going to start that now, eh?"

"Nah." She smiled again, looking across the lake, trying to hear his footsteps over the crash of the surf. He was notoriously light-footed, and one of the few people in this town she could trust. Only six weeks ago they had been equals, before her father-in-law died and left the Sheriff's desk empty, and she took the interim position. Rankin was a better police officer, she knew. Better at procedure. Better with people. There was a sense of calm and safety about him. Maybe it was his size. Maybe his stillness. Maybe the kindness in his brown eyes. But Minna had the questions. She was suspicious. Pushy. He comforted victims. She caught perps. So, she got the promotion and the support from the department to run.

She had so many questions. Who was this woman? Whose daughter? Wife? Mother? How long had she been in the water? How did she get there? What happened to her leg? Minna hoped she was dead before the water got her. Minna had spent a lot of time in the last years thinking about what it would be like to bob in the middle of the lake, with no land in sight, just flat blue as far as she could see. To bob until she couldn't tread any longer, until her muscles gave out, and then that sinking, sucking, feeling as the water absorbed her.

It was anyone's guess how long the ME would take to get her answers, their backwater county not being high priority. All she would have for now is what she could pull together, and as interim sheriff all eyes were on her. Her father-in-law had been beloved: smart and kind, he'd bend over backward for victims and their families. She was filling big shoes.

The gray water was dotted with icebergs. The ice on the bay had only been broken for a week. She wondered if the woman had been trapped under it. If the coming of spring, the warming water, had brought her to the surface. If she wasn't looking for a woman who just went missing.

She turned from the water and looked at the spot on the beach where the body had been. She wished she'd had Rankin's pictures. The woman had looked good, but Superior was so cold. Perhaps her leg injury was from the pack ice. The sharp ice that pushed and stacked on each other like tectonic plates along the beach could certainly destroy a leg. This was a theory she could bring to the public, one that didn't involve mythic creatures from the bottom of the lake.

She squatted next to the outline of the body, the footprints of her coworkers, the flat slide of the backboard a ring in the snow. Remembering the splay of the woman's limbs, the purple of her lips and fingers, she promised the woman that she would solve this mystery. She wouldn't leave this woman's family wondering. She was about to stand when a glint caught her eye. She leaned closer; a shard of metallic gray was lodged in the stones that had been beneath the woman's damaged leg. She pulled gloves from her pocket and picked it up. It looked like a piece of a saw blade, or a shark's tooth. She put it in a plastic baggie. She searched the rest of the woman's impression but found no other foreign matter.

Minna stood on the shore, listening to the wind whistle past her ears, looking down at the gray triangle in her hand, and thought about the pictographs of the water lynx on the cliffs across the lake. She wasn't the first one to consider this beast. She thought of its sharp teeth, and claws, and the spikes that graced its back and remembered yet again why she stayed out of the deep.

Then

Snow was falling from the flat gray sky in fat clumps. They stuck to Minna's eyelashes as she lifted her face and stuck out her tongue to catch them.

"Is that supposed to be Mishipeshu?" Chris asked, brushing his mittens together and stepping away from his snowman version of Gordie Howe.

"Yep, but I can't get the spikes on her back to stand up."

"We could knock some of the icicles off the garage and use those."

The two kids charged over to the garage and stared up at the jagged ice dangling from the roofline.

"There's got to be a stick, a shovel, or something in the garage that we can knock them down with," he said.

They went into the garage and while Chris looked for something with a long handle, Minna looked up to the rafters.

"What about that," she said pointing high up on the wall.

"My grandpa's old saw. He and his brother used it to clear this land. They each held the side and yanked."

"It's perfect," Minna said. "I want a closer look." She turned over a bucket and used it to climb up onto the freezer. The saw looked exactly like the water lynx's pine in her mind, long and flexible.

"That would look cool," he said, climbing up beside her.

"What the hell are you two doing?" Chris's dad asked from the door. He was still in his uniform. His new sheriff badge winked at Minna and she swallowed hard. "Minna sweetheart come down from there," he said, holding his arms out to her so she could jump. "You two know not to play around freezers. This one locks on its own. If you ever ended up inside you wouldn't get out. And Jesus, Chris you know that, how many times have I told you these aren't toys. You could lose your hand if you touched them wrong," he hollered, pointing at the collection of traps hanging from the wall. Minna knew not to touch them. Her dad had some at home.

She had seen him catch a coyote once. Her stomach turned at the thought of the sounds that animal had made before Daddy shot him.

"Minna, sweetheart, can you go get in the cruiser? Another person's gone missing, and it's not safe for you to be out. I'm going to take you back to your mom on my way back to work. Chris, you go on inside. Your mother is waiting."

Minna climbed into the passenger seat of the cruiser. There was a paper bag sitting on the floor with a loaf of bread sticking out of the top.

"Buckle up," he said. "That's for you and your mama, okay?" he pointed at the bag. Chris's daddy's car was just the same as her daddy's, but it smelled of cologne and peppermints, while her daddy's smelled like salt and Christmas trees.

"I know your mama is really angry right now, and she has every right to be. And I know that she doesn't want to talk to me. But you know if you ever need anything you just call, eh? Your daddy was my best friend, and I'll do anything for you."

"Is," she said.

"Sorry, love?"

"Is your best friend. He'll be home soon."

Now

The bell above the door jangled as Minna stepped into Pour Boys and knocked the slush off her boots. John was behind the bar. He waved, and pointed toward the back corner. She nodded her thanks. Chris was waiting for her, a Bell's in front of him, and a Coke waiting for her. She knew as soon as she sat, Susie, John's wife, would put plates of fried walleye and French fries in front of them. Her stomach grumbled with anticipation. She'd spent a long day looking for more gray triangles on the beach, and leaving harassing voice messages for the ME. She slid into the booth and smiled at her husband.

"Hey baby," he said, putting his phone down. "Found Mishipeshu?"

"I'm not in the mood to be poked."

Chris raised his eyebrows. Normally she would smile, but she was too tired.

"I'm being serious," he said. "You know we've talked about this for decades, you know how I feel."

"I know. Sorry. It's just," she pulled her phone out of her pocket and swiped at the screen, "look at that bite on her leg. It's not a bear. It's not a sturgeon either."

Chris handed back her phone as Susie set the plates down. Minna was sure to tip the screen away from the waitress, aware that not everyone talked about bodies and wounds over dinner. Except maybe the interim sheriff, and the son of the former sheriff, who was also a world-class rescue diver.

"There's nothing in that bay that would have made those marks. That's for sure," he said, shoving fish into his mouth. "But we both know that there's plenty of predators out there."

Minna squeezed lemon on her fish, and bit her lip. He was right. She could have got that injury on land, but Lake Superior was full of secrets. Anyone who spent any real time on the water had stories, experiences that couldn't be explained any way other than a fantastic beast. Fisherman and sailors on freighters came to town with tales of boats being bumped, nets with holes larger than any fish ever caught. Her father had no respect for the environmentalists, but they had stories too of mutilated animal remains, fish and wildlife with horrible injuries. Every local family had a story. The lore ran deep. These bites were pointing to Mishipeshu, but would the beast have given this woman up? How had she gotten away? How was Minna going to explain her theory to the other officers and not get laughed out of town?

"How are you?" she said. "House cleaning still? Need some help?"

"God, he was a pack rat, there's something in every corner, every drawer is full of shit, from fishing lures to old mittens to receipts from lunches decades ago that I'm sure he had with your dad. Trophies and certificates, and pictures, so many pictures. But no, it's okay, it's kind of cathartic, saying goodbye to things he loved, things that meant something to him, getting to revisit all these memories, just me and him." He took a bite and chewed. "It will be really nice to get the house on the market and off our hands though. Clean slate, you know?"

Things hadn't been easy the last couple of years. Working for her father-in-law was a challenge, but he'd always been good to her. She suspected out of his love for her father, maybe out of guilt that he hadn't been able to find him or save him. She knew though that he'd hoped that Chris would do something bigger with his life. He hated him poking around the bottom of the lake, he said. Hated that they entertained the idea of Mishipeshu and called them old-fashioned.

"What's that?" she said pointing at a package sitting next to Chris in the booth.

"New weight belt," he said. "Getting too thick in the middle for my other one."

Her phone vibrated on the table. It was the ME. She didn't even wipe the grease from her fingers before she answered. But when the doctor gave her the news, it wasn't at all what she was expecting.

"You look like you've seen a ghost," Chris said as she put down the phone.

"I sort of have."

"What?" he said, laughing, taking a drink of his beer. "And people think we're crazy for believing in a water panther."

She shook her head. "It's the woman. They identified her. She's been missing for thirty years. It's her, Chris. It's the woman that disappeared when my dad did. Chris, everyone always said that they had been together. What if he's out there too?"

Then

Minna lay on the end of the dock peering down into the lake. There was ice on the wooden planks, and surrounding the post that went down into the water, but it would be more than a month before this bay would freeze. She had time.

"What are you doing kiddo?" Pappa asked, standing over her. "This isn't a safe place for you to be hanging out. I know you're a good swimmer, but your snowsuit and this cold water don't mix."

"I'm being careful. I need to see."

"See what?" he said, and bent over, looking into the water. "What is that down there? An anchor?"

"Coyote trap."

"What? How do you know? How did that get there?"

"I couldn't find the bear traps."

"You put that down there? Jesus, Minna! Someone is going to get really hurt."

"Not in the winter. No one's going down there in the winter. Except Mishipeshu. We're going to catch her, and then ask her where she took my dad."

"Oh Minna!"

"You said that's why we couldn't find him, because he was with her. That's why Lake Superior never gives back its dead. It's because of her, and I want him back."

Now

Minna pulled into the rutted drive and wished she'd brought Rankin with her. He was so much better at this kind of stuff than her. He knew what to say to grieving families. She just seemed to make it worse. But the notification was an hour from the station and they both couldn't be gone that long just for this. Someone had to hold down the fort. She closed the truck door and stamped her boots on the ground to warm her feet. A man came out of the open garage door.

"Can I help you?" he asked, his eyes running over her uniform.

"Are you Rebecca Whitefish's next of kin?"

"That's my mom. Did you find her?"

"Yes," she said.

"Wow," he said, stepping back into the garage and leaning on the edge of a saw horse. "I didn't expect that, not after all this time, not this way." He rubbed his face with his hands. "Wait. I heard on the news a body washed up on the beach, that's not her, is it? It can't possibly be, thirty years in the water...."

Minna nodded. "That's what we are investigating now. I'm sorry I don't have more answers. Will let you know, as soon as we know, but I thought you'd want the closure of at least knowing—"

"That she's dead. She isn't living in Detroit or Minneapolis. That's what the police tried to tell my grandfather."

"Can I speak to your grandfather?"

"He's dead, too."

"I'm very sorry to hear that." She took a deep breath. "And I'm very sorry that the police at the time were not as helpful as they could have been. I know there was a lot going on for them."

"It's not real comforting when your mom is missing though, yeah? Shit," he said and leaned harder into the sawhorse.

Minna turned to give him a minute to pull himself together and noticed a boat in the back of the garage covered with a tarp. Sky blue boat. A boat exactly the same color as her eyes.

"Where'd you get that?" she asked

"Sheriff gave it to my grandpa. Said it was to help with his environmental protection projects. Grandpa knew it was a bribe, or a warning maybe for him to stop making trouble with his protests."

"Protests?"

"All the waste from the paper plant used to be dumped into the lake. Decimated the fish population, which drove the predators into town because they're starving, but that's an excuse to trap those big beautiful beasts, isn't it? Anyway, because of my grandpa they don't dump or trap wolves or bears anymore."

"Which sheriff?"

He shrugged. "What does it matter?"

"After your mom went missing?"

He shrugged again. "I wasn't there. Mighta been before. Grandpa had a lot of run-ins with 'em. I just keep it because the police gave it to us, and they never did nothing else for us. Seems like maybe that means something."

"Can I look in there?" she asked.

His eyes narrowed. "You have a warrant?"

"It could be a crime scene."

"I don't think the police would give us a crime scene? Do you?"

He was right, there wouldn't be any blood evidence in there. She just wanted in to soothe the ache inside her. Maybe it would still smell like him. Maybe there would be some of his things. Her mother had been so angry, she hadn't kept anything.

"I'd like to see in it."

"No. I don't want you to find some reason to take it."

She could reveal herself. She could tell him that she was an orphan, too. That she was angry at the police, too. That she also lived in a state of constant hope that made her brittle and fragile. She could lay claim to this boat, but she'd compromise everything. She'd get a warrant. She'd come back.

She nodded, "I'm sorry for your loss. I'll be in touch with any further developments." She looked at the blue boat one more time. The one she knew said "Minnow" on the back, above the motor, and then she left wondering whether it was her dad or her father-in-law who gave the boat away, if her mother knew, and if this was why her father-in-law and mother hated each other.

Then

Despite the cold weather, Minna was sunburned. Her cheeks felt hot and tight. The feeling reminded her of fishing with her dad. She swallowed hard. They were headed back to land with a cooler full of fish. It had been a good day.

"I wish we were in your dad's boat," Chris shouted over the loud motor. "It's so much faster and nicer than my dad's. I just want to go home and eat."

"Yeah," she said, but she wasn't paying attention, she was scanning the surface of the water for swirls, or lumps, or anything out of the ordinary. Anything that could be the monster that took her father. And gripping the gunwale. She'd never been afraid of the deep water before, but when she looked down all she could imagine was beasts, lurking.

Chris's dad docked the boat, and the kids raced to shore to pee and warm up and then watch Inspector Gadget on the basement TV while the grownups dealt with the fish. Minna loved Penny. Chris said they looked alike. This was her favorite show, but she couldn't concentrate. She was so angry at her pappa for pulling that trap out of the water.

"You still thinking about Mishipeshu?"

"Always. I've realized I can't catch her, though. I have nothing big enough to get her inside. So, I'm going to bait her, if I could just get a picture of her, I'd have enough proof. Someone would believe me, and help."

"You just got to get a pile of fish. We could catch them."

"I can get it from the garbage at the market. My dad used to get his bait from there for his traps."

"You're gonna be just like Penny," Chris said.

She smiled, crossed her arms and sunk into the couch to watch the end of the episode.

"Minna," Chris's dad called down the stairs to the basement. "Time to go home sweetie and take that container with you, okay? Some of the fish we caught today."

"I don't know why you're sending so much," Chris's mom said. "It's just the three of them. Put the extra in the freezer in the garage."

"Because," Chris's dad said widening his eyes, "I'm not sure how she's paying the bills right now, you know."

"I'm not sure he's not in that kiln of hers. Have you checked there? The woman is a first-class bitch."

Minna hated when adults talked about her like she wasn't there, and since her dad disappeared it happened more and more. Rumors and guesses about where he'd gone, rhetorical questions about how the family was holding up, or making ends meet. But today it didn't matter. Minna had a bag of fish so big she could barely lift it, and she couldn't believe her luck.

Now

Minna was parked at the county boat launch, watching the water, remembering the look on her mother's face thirty years before when her father pulled that blue boat on its trailer into their yard. Disbelief, and then anger, and then screaming. He'd spent all their money, and money they didn't have. It had been the subject of a hundred arguments in the weeks preceding his disappearance. She was wondering how to ask her mother if she'd known about Rebecca's family having the boat when the ME's office called. She punched her steering wheel, and drove straight to the office. She needed Rankin's calm head, she was losing hers.

"Frozen," she said, slapping the desktop. "Fucking frozen like a goddamn lasagna."

"The water is very cold. The ice is just breaking up. She was probably trapped in the pack just like you thought."

"No like frozen in someone's freezer." She skimmed through the report on her phone while she talked. "Fish scales, deer DNA, and residues that are consistent with the plastic interior of a freezer."

"So not commercial then? Are most of them metal?"

"Jesus Christ. Some regular person had this woman in their home freezer for thirty years. And, and the punctures are from a bear trap." She collapsed into her desk chair. "You know the rumor right? Rebecca and my dad ran away together. That they took his boat and started a new life somewhere else, but instead her family has his boat and she's in a freezer."

"You think maybe her family didn't want them to be together, killed them both and hid the boat? Made up some story about it being a gift. It's a really generous gift."

Her head was hot, her stomach doing somersaults. Rankin continued: "Minna, what would your mom have done if she found out your dad gave that boat away?"

She rested her head on the desktop. She was thinking about her mother, and what she would have done if she'd found the two together. She couldn't imagine her mother not selling the boat if she had the chance, certainly she wouldn't give it to her husband's mistress. Her mother had been so angry for so many years. She'd been sure that her husband had abandoned them for that woman. Minna couldn't imagine the energy it would have taken to fake that. She knew her mother didn't have it. Minna felt a loosening in her neck muscles, relief. That left her father, and Chris's. She had a hard time imagining her father giving away his boat, he'd been so proud of it, but maybe if he'd run out of money, maybe Rebecca's son had been mistaken and his grandfather had bought the boat to use for his protests. Minna found herself wishing that the answer was as easy as Mishipeshu. It was so much simpler when she was a child and had something to blame, one easy target for her anger.

"What's our next step?" Rankin asked quietly. He would suggest action of course. "A warrant for the boat? Canvassing? Or waiting for more information on the metal?"

Minna lifted her head as her gut tightened into a knot. "I know whose freezer she's been in," she said. "I just need to know why."

Then

Chris was standing at her front door with an ice auger.

"I can't. I'm grounded."

"Still?"

"Still."

"Over the fish?"

"Yep. Wasting food, two weeks. Huge mess, two weeks."

"God, your mom is mean. You're grounded till Christmas! I thought we could go drill some holes and set some traps."

"I'm not allowed out."

"Am I allowed in?"

Minna thought back to her mother's red-faced instructions. She hadn't said anything about Chris coming over, and she wasn't home, and Pappa was asleep in front of the hockey game.

"Sure, but be quiet," she said and they tiptoed to her room and closed the door.

Chris pointed to her dad's work hat, laying on her bed. "You really miss him, eh?"

Minna picked up the hat and smelled it. "Yeah. And I'm going to be police when I grow up so I can find him. So, I've been wearing it to practice."

"Don't you think Mishipeshu has him? My dad's trying, he's working overtime, he's never home and he's crying a lot. My mom tells him he's working too much. I know if your dad was out there on land he'd find him."

"My mom says he left with that woman. Took his new fancy boat and his new fancy woman and split. So, I'll be like Inspector Gadget and find them. Plus, I can't look down the bottom of the lake, it's too deep."

"I could," he said. "I'd do that for you."

"It's so deep," she said. "It's dark and cold and she's down there, and people who go down there don't come back. I don't want you—" She burst into tears.

He wrapped his arms around her. "I'll do it right," he said. "I'll look and I'll come back. I'll find the answer. You don't have to do it alone."

Now

At first, she thought no one was there. His truck wasn't in the driveway. She was relieved that she was wrong, but then she opened the side door to the garage and found it, and Chris. He was wearing rubber gloves. The room smelled of bleach.

"Is my dad in that freezer?" she said, pointing to his father's game freezer.

He shook his head.

"Was he?"

Chris looked down at his hands. He nodded.

"Where is he now?"

"With Mishipeshu."

"What?"

"She was the first and I messed up. I thought she would sink and she didn't. I should have weighted her."

"But you knew better for the second time."

He nodded.

"How long have you known? Since we were kids?"

"No."

"I'm such a fool. I trusted your dad. I trusted you. You're the one who encouraged me to think it was that fucking monster all these years. And you knew!"

"No! I didn't. Not till Dad started to get sick. He knew he was going to die and his position was going to be open and he wanted me to join the police so I could run for it, and continue his legacy, but I didn't want to. I'm happy diving. I love it. He told me I was doing it out of loyalty to you, out of some misplaced sense of duty to a stupid fairy tale that you convinced me of, and that you were just as dumb as your father. And then he told me.

"Your dad and Rebecca weren't together. It was mine. He loved her. He was going to leave my mom. Your dad was trapping bears for their parts. For the money. That's how he could afford that boat.

Rebecca came from a family of conservationists. One night she went out in the woods to disable his traps, to ruin them, and she stepped in one. Our dads were together when they found her dead, your dad wanted to cover it up, wanted to bury her where he buried the remains of the bears. But my dad loved her and was so mad at your dad, and his stupid, greedy, traps, and what happened, that he killed your dad, and put both the bodies in the freezer. I'm so sorry Minna. I had no idea. When we were kids, he was so devastated, he was a mess, drinking all the time. I thought it was because your dad was missing. I had no idea it was this. I would have told you. Fuck, I wouldn't have spent my life searching the bottom of the lake."

Chris leaned against his truck. Pulled a rubber glove off and rubbed his hand through his hair. "But I kind of understand. If he loved her even half as much as I love you, I would kill anyone who hurt you, even my best friend.

"He was so ashamed. I think he would have taken the secret to his grave. He probably only told me because he was too weak to move the bodies and he knew he was going to be found out anyway. He probably wanted to defend himself. But what he did, it's indefensible. And all I've ever wanted was you, to protect you, to take care of you. I didn't want you to carry this. I thought this was better."

Minna watched his fingers, his hands, and how they grasped each other as he spoke, pleading for her to understand. How over the years, with those hands, he had held her, protected her, and helped her. She thought about how he pulled the flesh of

Rebecca, and her father from the freezer with those same fingers. How he had loaded them into his truck and then into a boat all by himself. All the work and care it would have taken, the burden that he had carried. How he had done it for her, to save her the pain of knowing how stupid her father's end had been. And she hurt for him, knowing not only had his father put him in this terrible position of knowing, but he had also stolen Chris's lifelong dream to find the monster in the water; instead, he'd been living with the monster all this time.

But still her trust had been broken, and she needed to know. She needed to see for herself.

"Take me," she said. "Take me down in the water where you dropped him. I need to see him."

"Minna, no. That's a terrible idea. It's so deep where I dropped him and you're a beginner and you're afraid of the deep. We won't be able to go far enough down to find him."

"I have to try. Thirty years, Chris. I've waited thirty years."

He sighed, and nodded, and they got their gear, and Chris's boat, and he brought her out to the deepest point of the lake. "It's 1,300 feet here. You can only go about fifty. So please don't expect anything."

"Maybe he got caught on something," she said, put in her mouthpiece and tipped backward into the water.

It was breathtakingly cold. Every muscle in her body contracted into a hard ball. She pushed through the cramps, trying to enjoy the quiet and the rhythm of her breath, trying not to think about the darkness below.

Chris signaled her and they began to descend slowly, her heart breaking a little with each foot of open water. It wasn't until she was nearing her limit of fifty feet that she saw rocky outcroppings. She pushed on. She could see Chris signaling, but she ignored him. More and more rocks appeared in the beam of her flashlight, but she saw nothing suspicious. It was darker and colder than she'd ever been, and she was angry and disappointed. She was just about to stop and return to the surface when she saw a flash of red in her beam, red like Chris's old weight belt, and she kicked down toward it, but it was gone. She kept descending, looking, sure she'd seen it. Pain built in her ears. Sparkles emerged in her vision, and she finally stopped. She'd lost Chris in her frantic swimming and was alone in the dark.

The weight of the lake was pressing down on her. Plus the weight of the knowledge of what their fathers had done, and the heavy realization that finding her father and knowing for sure was a lost cause; Superior didn't give up her dead.

She should swim, but her limbs wouldn't obey and she was so very tired.

She dropped the flashlight.

As it descended, the falling beam shining through the black water caught the flash of scales, and spines, and big intelligent eyes.

Author's note:

Growing up on a small island in the channel between Lake Huron and Lake Superior, the water, and the threat of it, was always a significant part of my life. I could look out my bedroom window and watch the freighters rumble past; Gordon Lightfoot's "The Wreck of the Edmund Fitzgerald" was a regular fixture on our soft rock station. Usually, the danger was the temperature, the ice, or being in too small a craft in the wrong kind of weather. But since it's well known that Superior "doesn't give up her dead" those of us with active imaginations might like to ignore the science of cold water and let them wander to Mishipeshu, the mythological water panther of the Anishinaabe, which is where this story was born.

CLIFFS OF BLOOD
ZAKARIAH JOHNSON

AS IF SENSING THE WOMEN would happily convert them into potions, the sidewinders and other creatures gliding through the desert night steered clear of the trio as they wound their way up the scree-covered slope of Vermillion Mesa. Permits were required to enter the Cliffs of Blood National Monument, and they did not have one. While the paperwork wasn't impossible to obtain, the deciding issue behind Nin, Shelby, and Ashley's illegal entry was that all their birth names and several aliases tended to trigger flashing lights and jangling sirens inside the headquarters of numerous three-letter agencies, so they tried their best to stay out of the system.

The first full moon after the spring equinox had risen two weeks before, signaling the beginning of mating season on the mesa. The first kits would already have been born, making the mothers edgy and dangerous. But it wasn't the jills—as females of the species are known—that worried the women as much as the jacks. Deep into the rutting season, the jacks' testosterone-addled brains had space for only two imperatives: mate and vanquish. Nin had warned the others that, as Homo sapiens, their detection would only inspire violence.

"Wait!" Nin hissed as a flash of electricity burst overhead. Behind her, Shelby and Ashley looked up, bug-eyed in their night-vision goggles that outlined Nin's body in green-and-black. A clap of thunder boomed though the air, triggering a miniature rockslide beside them. Nin counted silently to twenty before she spoke again. "Don't. Make. A sound."

Storm clouds were gathering fast over the mesa, obscuring the risen moon and northeast Arizona's famous wheel of desert stars. Another flash of light lit the underside of the billowing mass before everything dropped into darkness. The flashes appeared white in the night-vision goggles, though the women knew they were really a vivid blue. They longed to see the unfiltered light, but beneath the clouds they couldn't have seen their hands in front of their faces or the protective crystals dangling from each other's necks without goggles or flashlights. And carrying flashlights would be suicide.

Nin signaled a huddle. "Remember, if they butt heads, look away fast or your night vision's shot. Got it?" The acolytes both nodded. "Shelbs?"

"It's here," she whispered, reaching into her collecting basket woven from yucca and devil's claw fibers to retrieve an obsidian blade hafted onto a human thigh bone. The knife was for harvesting any Welsh's milkweed they found—an herb useful in several concoctions which even the Pentagon's paranormal weapons program, "The Pentagram," didn't know about, or so Nin had assured them. Nin, aka Colonel Belit, would surely know, having risen to the number three spot in the organization before being court-martialed for theft. Shelby's obsidian blade could also kill and skin any newborns if they found a den. Shelby had briefly wondered if she could kill a kit, but she'd been taught that the animals weren't sentient, plus she figured she'd disemboweled a hundred chickens in her day so what was the difference? A much larger flash than before lit up the underside of the clouds, followed by a boom that fluttered Shelby and Ashley's long hair and shook even Nin's mousse-encrusted flattop.

"The jacks are fighting. Let's go," Nin said, then turned and crept the last twenty feet to the mesa's rim.

Dressed in black yoga pants, a black hoodie, and rubber-soled shoes like the others, Ashley, a first-degree acolyte, brought up the rear. She'd assumed the heavy-set Shelby, a second-degree, would be the one to lag behind, but the big woman had put her to shame despite the extra weight she carried. Nin had already reprimanded Ashley for panting so loud on the way up, and she paused to catch her breath as the silhouettes of the other two women slipped over the edge of the mesa. Ashley knew she was the weak link here, knew she kept herself trim not through exercise but via a steady regimen of amphetamines and dissipation. If she hadn't gotten stoned at the music festival, her hook-up for the night wouldn't have been able to make off with the coven's antler necklace they'd entrusted her with—the amulet the three had come to replace. Ashley still had the second one though, and as long as she wanted it, she mused, no one could make her take it off, not even Nin.

As Ashley pulled herself onto the mesa top, she saw Nin and Shelby crouched behind a bush. Shelby peered over the rocky field while Nin pulled the bottle of thirty-year-old lowland Scotch out of her own gathering basket.

"I'll uncork it once the traps are set," Nin said. "One whiff and every jack on the mesa will stampede us." She reached into the bag again and pulled out two rabbit-traps with silver-coated teeth and a mallet for hammering their anchors into the red sandstone underfoot.

"It looks clear," Shelby whispered, lowering her night-vision binoculars and resetting her goggles over her eyes. "I saw some bugs fluttering by that outcrop. I think they're owlet moths—that means milkweed in bloom." Basket in one hand, knife in the other, she set off without waiting permission.

"Thirty minutes! No more, no less," Nin hissed after Shelby's vanishing back. "Get out the hacksaw, Ashley."

Ashley slipped off her hip canteen and took a long drink before following orders. The unnatural clouds above held no rain and the desert winds were hot and desiccating. Plus, screw Nin anyway, she thought. What did a third-degree mistress need her help for anyway, it wasn't like she'd lost the amulet on purpose or—

"Any time now," Nin said, bringing Ashley out of her reverie. She hoped Nin hadn't read her mind. She put away the canteen and retrieved her hacksaw. They'd coated the blade with silver, a requirement for cutting through the creature's antlers. These weren't Wyoming tourist-trap curios they were after, not the kitschy make-believe sold at Little America or hung over the bar at Bronco Billy's saloon. This was the real deal: *Lepus temperamentalus*, "the warrior rabbit," the North American jackalope, whom they'd come to harvest in body and power. And the bunnies don't play.

Nin did a chin point to the next outcrop, then darted off, crouching low and moving fast. Following her, Ashley worked hard not to stumble, fearing embarrassment as much as Nin's retribution. When Nin crouched behind a small boulder, Ashley didn't need orders to follow suit.

"Look," Nin said, pointing across the mesa. "Take off your goggles. It's glorious."

Ashley lay prone beside her instructor and did as told, squinting into the darkness. About 100 yards distant, a blue light sparkled. Then another, followed by the crackling of electricity rolling over the ground.

"That's a harem with five or six jills," Nin said. "The males that were fighting earlier must be there!"

Outlined in the blue light that swirled over the smaller antlers of the female jackalopes, two stout males squared off, waggling their massive crowns of antlers. The challenger began thumping his foot like a drummer breaking in a new bass pedal. The second jack, master of the harem, responded, his back foot pounding the ground, blue light crackling over the massive rack he began tilting toward his foe.

"Those are as big as moose antlers!" Ashley whispered in greed and awe, resetting her goggles.

Nin grinned. "Hope your sawing arms are ready for a workout—close your eyes!" Nin ducked her head as she said it, clapping her palms tight over her ears.

The electricity swirling around the jacks' heads suddenly swelled in brightness, the blue orbs nearly encompassing them as they lowered their heads and rushed each other. Hitting, the collision discharged a shockwave that swept the mesa in a blinding flash of blue light and deafening thunder. This was the power the women sought. When a pair of antlers from any two jackalopes are struck together, the explosion—properly directed—can stun humans for miles away. It can sink a ship, trigger an avalanche, bring down a plane.

Ashley did not close her eyes in time.

Meanwhile, Shelby had tracked the swarm of owlet moths she knew were the prime pollinators for the endangered Welsh's milkweed. She followed the insects past a boulder outcrop, down a gulley, then around another pile of rocks before finding the flowering plants she was seeking.

"Come to mama," she whispered, sniffing in a breath of their heady scent.

She donned a pair of rubber kitchen gloves and began slicing the flowers off mid-stem with her obsidian blade, determined to harvest them all if she could. The plant was endangered, but to her, its immediate usefulness outweighed concerns over its extinction. As a prominent member of the FBI's Most Wanted occult list, Shelby had her own extinction to worry about. She lopped off one flowering bunch after another, dropping them into the basket without letting her skin touch them. Reaching for the last, she glanced down and noticed a dim glow emitting from the underside of the flat stone on which she stood. She silently set down the basket, stepped gingerly off her perch, and circled around toward the light. Something inside a tiny den beneath the rock was definitely glowing. She slipped her goggles over her forehead for a better look. Yes, the light was blue, but softer than the flashes they'd seen earlier. She reached in and pulled back the milkweed roots hanging down from the roof of the den and saw them. Four tiny newborns, hairless and blind, wriggled beside each other in a bed of dry milkweed leaves. On their naked heads, Shelby could see the black buds of their incipient horns. Four jackalopes. Four sets of horns. They were small, but powerful. With one bud fitted into each of a pair of bracelets, the wearer would never fear being apprehended, let alone disobeyed. Just slap the buds together and—boom!

As she watched, the soft blue light swirled and crackled in the den, releasing a brief scent of ozone.

"Can you do this?" she asked herself, then giggled at the pretense, "Yeah, girl. You can." With the hand holding the obsidian blade, she tugged to double-check that the rubber glove on her other hand was on tight, then reached for the first baby.

"Ouch," she said.

The first shock was tiny, like the jolt your stupid brother might give you after dragging his socks over the carpet. An instant later, she found herself flying backward through the air like she'd pissed on the third rail in the subway, her chest split open by a massive blue bolt that burned the remaining flesh from her bones before she hit the ground.

"Can you see yet?" Nin asked Ashley, who sat holding her goggles.

"Yeah. Kinda. I guess," she said, blinking away the spots dancing before her eyes. Touching a hand to her bleeding ear, she asked, "Was there an echo? I thought I heard two blasts. I think my eardrum's busted."

"Well, suck it up, buttercup," Nin said. "It'll be a lot worse for you if we go back empty-handed. The council wanted to execute you until I talked them out of it. Yeah. That's right. So, grin and bear it and let's do this." Nin looked up and saw the jacks preparing for another joust. She used their distraction to risk hammering the first trap's anchoring spike into the rock. Trap anchored, she pulled back the springs to set it and then tore the wrapper off the whiskey bottle.

"As soon as I pore this, they'll smell it and come running. Get behind a rock and wait. Got your mace?"

"Yeah, I got it," Ashley nodded, pulling the steel-headed, medieval club from her pack. Its thirteen ridges were also glazed in silver, not to mention poison.

"Good girl. Remember what Shelby coated it with. Don't screw up." With that, Nin poured a dram of whiskey into the basin welded in the middle of the trap, recorked the bottle, and hustled off to set the second device.

Alone now and on her knees behind a boulder, Ashley craned her head around the rock to check where the harem had been, but there were no lights to be seen. "Don't screw up," she mimicked Nin, now that the elder was gone.

"Don't screw up," said a voice behind her. Spinning fast, Ashley faced a line of five jills staring back at her.

"Don't screw up," said the center one in a perfect imitation of Nin's voice. "Don't screw up," said another. Then another. The row of females, lit by the electricity of mating season swirling through their smaller antlers, repeated the phrase over and over, talking all at once and over each other.

They're mimics, Ashley reminded herself. Like parrots. They don't know what they're saying.

"Ouch!" one of the jills said, jerking back her forepaw in a show of pain as she did so. Her voice sounded like Shelby's.

"Ouch!" said another, mimicking the same injury with her paw.

"Ouch!" "Ouch!" "Ouch!" "Ouch!" "Ouch!"

Saying "ouch" once more, the center jill curled back her harelips to reveal her massively oversized top teeth and grinned.

Ashley swung the silver-coated mace with all her might, hoping to brain the cheeky beast. As the club came down, the jill jumped aside, then vanished. The others followed suit, lunging and darting, disappearing and reappearing as they bounded around her, blinking in and out of existence like a glitching computer screen. She felt something scrape her leg, cutting through her yoga pants and scratching the skin below.

"Oh crap," she said, remembering Nin's warning about the poisoned blades. The jackalopes stopped hopping, becoming still at the five points of a star around her and watching as the weapon slid from her hand and she sank to her knees. She tugged the necklace bearing her remaining tine of jackalope antler from under her shirt and held it out as a talisman to fend them off. Feeling her limbs grow cold, the antler slipped from her fingers as she fell face-first onto the ground.

"I'll take that," a voice said. Ashley felt impossibly soft hands brushing her neck as someone worked the necklace's clasp free and released it. Her final thought was a smug triumph: Jackalopes were "non-sentient" they'd said. Ha! Nin hadn't been so smart after all...

Nin stood over the smoking skeleton of the second-degree witch formerly known as Shelby. The smell of charred intestines was dreadful, but she'd smelled worse. Nin didn't consider the younger witches' deaths a betrayal, because she'd never really joined their coven. Nin had prior loyalties, and those always took precedence.

"You came through," said a voice behind her in the darkness. She knew better than to turn around.

"I pay my debts. Here's the other half." She reached into her hoodie's pocket and pulled out the coven's second stolen antler, the bit thought to have been filched by Ashley's one-night stand. The figure behind her lifted it from Nin's hand without touching her.

"And the whiskey?"

Nin laughed. "Always the whiskey with you guys."

She uncorked the bottle and took a swig, feeling the long tail of the premium Scotch slide down her throat. She recorked the bottle and held it out behind her. A fur-covered hand that seemed nearly human brushed over hers as it took the offering.

"So, you've got the trophies back. What about your half of the bargain?" Nin asked. "The Pentagram's price for maintaining and protecting this refuge?"

"We're like you, Colonel Belit. We do what it takes to survive," said the jackalope, pausing to take a deep swallow of whiskey. "Next time your government needs a storm, you know where to find us."

Author's note:

Some would have us believe the earliest known reference to jackalopes dates from only the 1930s, when transparently fake taxidermied heads of jackrabbits sporting deer antlers or antelope horns began popping up as tourist kitsch in Wyoming. However, horned leporids (the family including rabbits and hares) were described by Western science as early as the 1788 Tableau encyclopédique et méthodique and in Persian manuscripts as early as the thirteenth century (see "al-mi'raj" or "almiraj"). These earlier exposés suggest that folk wisdom regarding the cryptid's magical powers long predates its twentieth-century media boom. (After all, what self-respecting witch could resist experimenting with something as rare and elusive as rabbit horn?) At least some of these "horns" are now known to be caused by a variant of the papilloma virus. But are all of them? The vox populi remains unconvinced.

The reputed powers of jackalopes in first-hand accounts vary, though persistent traits include their gluttony for whiskey, that they mate during lightning flashes (which resemble their horns), their ability to mimic human speech, and especially their will-o'-the-wisp-like elusiveness—and menace—all of which come into play in "Cliffs of Blood." The impetus for "Cliffs of Blood" came from a visit to the Vermillion Cliffs National Monument, a 280,000-acre wilderness preserve adjacent to the Navajo Nation in NE Arizona. This preserve is among those that outgoing US presidents are in the habit of setting aside as their legacies, often with the result that their successors get petty and rescind the orders. But in cases where presidents DON'T scrub out each other's legacy monuments, such uncharacteristic magnanimity begs the question: Why were these monuments retained? "Cliffs of Blood" answers that.

HAENEYO
T.A. SIMONELLI

KIM FEEDS THE THING in the basement tank once a week. Two descaled and gutted flounder, one squid, head cavity emptied, and three long stalks of kelp that she goes to the water's edge to collect. She's never seen the thing; the tank water is always too murky and deep to catch more than flashes of something against the glass, and once, when she asked, her mother had told her it was because it liked it that way. She was three the last time her mother changed the water, and she wasn't allowed to watch. Too dangerous. She's sixteen and her mother is gone now, claimed by the sea, and her father refuses to go into the basement. That leaves the care and feeding of the thing to Kim.

Her mother never left instructions, not written down, not for anything that Kim didn't witness her doing with her own eyes. She didn't even keep a recipe book. Kim had to work from muscle memory to make her mother's kimchi and kamja guk, emulating motions that her mother had done countless times in front of her, and her versions were never quite right. Kim descended the stairs, bowl in hand, and pulled the cord to illuminate the thousands and thousands of pounds of tank that filled more than half the basement. The bulb didn't flicker to life, so she set the bowl down and pulled out her phone, three quick taps illuminating a beam across the room. She saw something twitch through the water, hiding from her, as she removed the lid from the ceramic bowl and set it aside. She always had this feeling of being watched when she fed the thing. Like she was being hunted, this creature taking as many opportunities to use its predatory instincts as it possibly could in captivity.

She scooped the squid up with her hands, stepping up the ladder carefully to the top of the tank and lifting the hatch with her elbow. She dropped the squid in and dropped the hatch in the same motion, a dull plunk sound echoing through the basement before a thrashing splash, and then the squid was gone. She scooped a flounder up and went to repeat the pattern, the same as every week.

Her father, Jun-Il, didn't talk about the tank in the basement. As far as he was concerned, it didn't exist. Sometimes though, Kim would wake up in the night and find the basement door open, her father standing in the center of the basement staring at the tank, watching the water for a sign. When she was a child, Kim had thought the thing inside was a beautiful mermaid, or a sea goddess, bringing good luck and blessings by living with them. As she dropped the second flounder into the hatch, she thought this could only be a curse. Fishy hands every day despite only feeding it once a week. It never fully washed off. Second-guessing and worrying about the tank during storms. It was like she had her own invalid child that couldn't survive without her there.

College was a distant dream to her, something that she thought of fondly, and worked toward, but knew the hard facts. She couldn't take the tank with her; as long as the thing in the tank was still there she would have to stay too. That's why she'd stopped feeding it every day, only once a week. It didn't seem to matter how little food it got. She fed it once a week for three years and it still survived, still held on to life and had the vigor to keep splashing her with brackish murky water every time she fed it. Kim dropped the kelp into the water and, instead of dropping the hatch, watched the water. The curve of an arm broke the surface and grabbed the kelp, yanking it down into the murk, the unnatural greenish tint making Kim shudder. She'd seen bits of it here and there, the dull scales, the razor teeth, the green skin. How sailors had been able to lust after them like they did she'd never know. As a kid she'd thought it was beautiful but as time went on, she found it more and more grotesque.

Kim's phone rang suddenly and slipped from her hand, plopping into the grimy water and sinking to the bottom.

"No!" she yelped and, unthinking, reached out to try and catch the phone. Her arm entered the water for just a moment before she yanked it back, webbed and clawed hands following it out. More than two, five hands reached from the depths of the tank and Kim fell backward off the ladder, yelling for her mother who had been dead for five years, as her head cracked back on the cement floor.

When Kim came to, her phone was lying cracked and waterlogged on the cement beside her face. It was obviously dead but light still shone from somewhere else in the room. Kim sat up and felt the back of her head, damp but not sticky from blood, and looked around, eyes finally falling on the tank. Lights danced inside, swirling and spinning around each other, and Kim leaned forward, planting a hand against the six-inch-thick glass only to startle when another hand, the size of a six-year-old's, with small bioluminescent spots, pressed against the other side. Kim pulled away from the glass and scrambled upstairs, slamming the door behind her.

It took four days for her to go back into the basement. When she did she took a floodlight along with a new bulb for the basement light. The lights were enough to keep the things from glowing in the tank as Kim inspected it. She walked around it, the same as she had done when she was a child a million times. Something was following her as she moved; she could see the edges of the plants in the tank swaying as they were brushed aside. Kim stopped and faced the tank, digging in her pocket. Her mother had told her to only condition the tank water when algae started to build up, but without sunlight there could be no algae. She approached the ladder and something thumped against the glass, making her drop the flashlight she had borrowed from their neighbor. She took a breath and grabbed it, directing the beam at the tank. Three small hands were against the glass, the water too murky to see anything more than scrawny, scaly arms vanishing into the water.

Kim swallowed thickly and climbed the ladder, dropping the water conditioning pellet into the tank, then backing up away from the tank. She sat on the floor and watched as the pellet fizzed, bubbles clearing away the murk and leaving the water a milky white rather than its normal swamp green. Then she saw them. The largest one, the one her mother had always taken care of, was missing an arm, parts of some of the plants and decorations in the tank wrapped around the stump, scales dim and frayed. The two smaller creatures were a surprise. There had only ever been one before; how she could have possibly managed to give birth without having been out of the tank? The two creatures were small, scrawny, looked to be maybe the equivalent size of a six-year-old human child from the waist up, with the dewy black dots of a deep sea eel going up each arm and down to the fins of their tails.

Kim had never seen them this clearly before. Her mother had warned that cleaning the tank too often would cause problems, but after ten years of not doing it Kim had no idea when to do it next, so she simply never had.

"Hi," Kim said softly, unsure what to do. The mother turned abruptly and looked at her through the glass, her shark-like skin shimmering with the sudden movement. The children twined through the tank toward the front of the tank. Kim swallowed. The children looked so different from their mother, her skin like that of a shark, sort of jagged and rough at the edges, complexion a sickly moonish green, her tail sharp at the fins like something built for chasing and devouring prey. The children were soft, almost jelly-like in the torso, small glowing spots along their body drowned out by the lights she'd put up in the room, their tails long and sinuous like an eel rather than any fish she'd seen before. The mother looked down at the small creatures then back at Kim and pointed to its mouth, shivers running up Kim's back at the sight of the thousands of small, razor sharp teeth.

Kim turned and grabbed the bucket of chum she'd bought off the neighbor and approached the hatch again. When she opened the hatch to pour it in one of the kids splashed her playfully. She smiled a little and poured the chum, all of the creatures voraciously attacking the fish guts as if they hadn't eaten in months. The mother rested on the bottom of the tank as the two kids played above her and Kim sat.

"You've been waiting a long time to give birth," Kim said and watched her eyes rise to meet hers, then looked behind her to the stairs. Kim turned and looked but nothing was there. Then things clicked. "You want out?"

There was a slam against the tank and the mother was there, her fist planted against the glass, a snarl on her face. She gestured toward the kids then back to the stairs and slammed against the tank with her shoulder, beating it with her fist until she was exhausted and floated back down to the bottom, covering her face with her hand, hunched over on herself. Kim backed away from the tank, grabbing both the flashlight and the floodlight, and ran toward the stairs. That night she could hear an occasional banging coming from deep beneath the house.

The tub wasn't that hard to get ahold of, the hydraulic lift was the harder thing to explain away. Her father had taken one look at the credit card statement and known something was amiss. She told him it was to move the piano from her room down to the living room, but he could tell, somehow he'd always been able to read her. He had spent more time down in the basement, despite the water in the tank almost overnight becoming the swamp murk that was familiar in the tank. If it wasn't for the occasional swish of her tail against the glass it was almost the same mystery that had always haunted her as a child, a mermaid in a tank. Kim could tell he was trying to stop what was inevitable, to hold on to that part of her mother that remained, but she couldn't let that happen. The banging had gotten worse as the days went on, keeping her awake at night, and the kids were getting smaller. There was only so many times she could ask the neighbors for extra scraps of fish, and they wouldn't eat it if it didn't come from the ocean.

She claimed a cold to stay home and her father looked at her with a sadness that she didn't expect. He told her to be careful, take care of herself, and then kissed her forehead, something he hadn't done since she was small, since her mother had died. Then he left, closing the door, locking up behind him, and drove away. Kim threw the blankets off after an eternal twenty minutes and ran downstairs, not even bothering to change into real clothes. She put the lift on top of the tank and lowered the strap down into the bottom as she scooped water from the tank into the tub. One of the kids went first, looping the strap around its gelatinous body and being lifted from the water. Kim lowered him carefully into the tub and then wrapped the strap around the tub with him safely inside. He thrashed for a moment until the mother slammed her hand against the tank and he looked at her. Kim had the lift help her get him up the stairs and then shoved the tub from one side of the kitchen to the other and out the back door. It had been stormy the last few days and the ocean reflected that, waves cresting high and falling hard back down onto the beach, foam and spray filling the air.

Kim dragged the tub to the edge of the water, her muscles screaming with exertion, her back and shoulders feeling like they were burning as she bent and pulled, bent and pulled. She stood straight and it felt like something her body was no longer capable of doing properly, a small stoop still in her stance. She removed the lid to the tub and the boy lifted his head from the water. He looked around and saw the ocean, his eyes going wide before barking a noise at her, a sort of hybrid of seals barking and electricity zapping through the air. Kim pushed the tub over, emptying the water and the contents into the surf. Before she could even stand back up he had crawled into the water and made his way almost farther out than she could see. She turned and dragged the tub back into the house, and started again.

The sun was almost down when she stood in front of the tank with the mother staring out at her, face pressed against the tank, her webbed hand spread wide on the glass. Kim stared into the tank, her arms and legs feeling like they were made of the same jelly that the boys had been made of. The mother slammed herself against the tank, over and over, screaming soundlessly from inside the tank as Kim set the tub to the side and sat down on the floor, staring at her. Purplish blood started clouding the tank and Kim set her hand against the tank.

"Shh, calm down, it's okay now," she whispered to the tank, the mermaid calming and staring back at her with horror and fear on her face. Kim shook her head and gestured to the stairs.

"You're next, I promise," she said softly.

She barely fit in the tub, her fins crimped by the lid as Kim closed it. She thrashed and pushed at the lid, trying to force it off as Kim moved her, dragging her across the compacted sand toward the surf. She burst through the lid halfway and Kim had to force her back into the tub before she dumped it yards from the shoreline. Kim got her to where the others had been dumped and the water swirled up around her ankles, the tide starting to come in. In the distance she could see the two glowing spots of the boys and threw the lid farther up on the shore, the mother crawling out and clawing back toward the house.

"What are you doing?" she yelled over the sound of the wind blowing in from the ocean. The mother screamed, trying to move her body back up to the house with a single arm. Kim grabbed her hand, rough shark skin digging into her hand, slick blood drenching her and making her slide through her hands. The mermaid screamed again and Kim slapped her, pointing out at the sea.

"They're waiting for you!" she screamed and the mermaid shook her head, looking back to the house, tearing at her lank hair with her one hand. "Just go!"

The mermaid looked at her and pressed a hand to Kim's chest, the area where she touched her skin feeling like fire and bleeding like she'd been punctured by hundreds of tiny needles. She turned and started throwing herself toward the ocean, moving quickly like a seal but hampered by her missing arm. Kim grabbed the tub and scrambled out of the water, watching her rush to her children. She waited a moment, expecting them to swim away and when they didn't she left, dragging the empty tub back toward the house, blood dripping from her hands. She threw the tub in the corner of the kitchen and went to the sink, rinsing her hands until the water finally ran clear. Then she sat at the kitchen table and waited for her father to get home so she could tell him that it was done, that they were all gone now and they didn't have to keep looking back. She could go to college, he could move away from this house if he wanted. Everything was different now. As tears finally started to prick at her eyes her head fell onto the table.

"I'm sorry umma," she whispered to the empty room, the empty house.

Then she heard the banging.

She walked slowly down the stairs, her hands bleeding again, and leaned against the entry to the landing when she spotted it. She was small, half the size of her brothers, still growing it seemed based on the size of her tail in proportion to her torso. She looked like a proper mermaid in miniature, small child breasts, smoothly scaled emerald green tail, a halo of vibrant red hair compared to the dull black luster of her shark mother. She looked exactly as Kim had imagined when she was a child and vanished so easily into the less murky tank's foliage. Kim fell onto her knees, tears growing in her eyes. Had her mother looked like this before? Before Kim's mother left her to take care of them, with no way to know how?

Kim sat for a long time crying in front of the tank, watching the little mermaid swim rapid, frantic circles around the tank.

Then she decides what she wants to do, and when her father finally gets home late from work, he helps her.

They clean the tank.

Author's note:

I wrote this story to be a sort of reflection on how cycles can repeat within a family, regardless of how much a person may try to prevent that, and how things that start out beautiful can be twisted and made into something corrupted from its original form. Cryptids have always felt like an exercise in forced perspective to me, a warped mirror laid against society and the things we fear most, and in the case of mermaids, that fear has always been one of the unknown and depths, how things become twisted beyond human understanding when placed just to the left of what human experience is. I have always been drawn to mermaids in the darker sense of the myth, creatures that sing sailors to doom and are more monster than human, flitting down in the depths of the ocean far beyond what human eyes can reach, until they get hungry. They're vengeful and angry, and it felt right to write a story that showed them as the fierce animals they can be.

THE VALLEY WHERE THE FOG HAS HOOVES

J.S. MCQUEEN

I AM SITTING ON THE FOREST FLOOR, hearing the sound of hoofbeats rushing through the valley for the first time. I am terrified. I think a herd of horses must be about to trample me because it sounds real and like it is heading directly for me. The wind passes over me and blows my hair back, and the sound drains into the valley behind me. It goes to the silence.

I wake up at home. I am not sure if I was dreaming because it felt so real. I resolve to go to the valley in search of the noise again.

It was one week before I heard the horses for the first time. I was making breakfast for myself and my father, who had just finished shambling into the front of the house in his underwear and walking up to me and putting his hands on my shoulders and kissing me on the top of the head. I thought to myself, for the first time, that I wished my mother were here to make breakfast instead. Then I thought to myself that I would never have a mother here to make breakfast instead. I had to excuse myself to the bathroom. I did not want to cry in front of him because if I did he would ask what's wrong.

Our house has three rooms, plus the bathroom, plus the living room and the kitchen. The entire house is covered in a short blue carpet that burns if you sit on it too much. The living room connects to the bedrooms through a hallway. My bedroom is at the end of that hallway to the right, and it is filled with all of the things my father couldn't not buy. His bedroom is on the other side, and it has only one bed and a dresser for his clothes. Neither of us go into the third room anymore. It was my mother's room.

I go to the valley in search of the sound a second time one week after the first. I have to sneak out at midnight to do it because my father does not like me leaving the house except to go to school. But after he takes his medication, which he sometimes does not do if I do not make sure he does, he will not wake up again. I made sure he did, so I open the window at midnight and slip out of it. I close it behind me. It is a fifteen-minute walk through the dark, smothered trails of the forest to get to the valley. I am not scared because I am used to it. When my eyes adjust, the light of the moon is enough. The forest smells like earth and pollen. I spend the time thinking about how I will tell everyone about the sound, and I remember my grandmother telling me the stories about the horses when I was a kid; we were still able to go and visit her back then. I think to myself that I wish I could tell grandma about the horses. I do not think to myself that I will never be able to tell grandma about the horses.

I arrive at the spot where I thought I heard the sound before, and I am relieved that the spot exists because I think if I had dreamed the spot then I wouldn't be able to find it. I sit and wait for the sound for a long time, but nothing happens. I go home. The fact that I found the same spot I was in before is enough to convince me to try again later.

Two years before I searched for the sound a second time, I looked in my mother's room. It felt like I was breaking a rule, but it looked like a normal bedroom to me, except it had more stuff in it than my room had. I thought to myself that I wish I could have stuff. I thought to myself that my mom must have had money to buy things because my father was always saying he didn't have money to buy anything for me. The thought that my mom might buy me things my father can't was exciting to me. I did not think to myself that I will never have a mother to buy me things.

Six months before I looked for the sound a second time, I went into my mother's room. I got her clothes out of her closet and tried them on, but they were too big for me. It did not feel like they should be too big for me. I wondered why couples on television slept in the same room but my parents slept in different rooms. I put them away carefully and never went into my mother's room again.

When an adult has a room, it becomes full of secrets. I think that is why it feels weird to go inside their rooms when they are somewhere else.

It has been seven weeks since I went looking for the sound and could not find it. I am back in the valley, not because I am looking for the sound but because I am angry and do not want to be in the house with my father anymore. I sit in the spot crying for hours. The hoofbeats begin in the distance, and I immediately stop crying and jump to my feet. They are coming toward me. And I am scared because it is really hard to remember that there are not horses when you are actually hearing it. The sound passes through me, and I run to follow it, but the forest is tricky, and I trip, and the sound fades away into the distance again. I do not care. I am smiling; the hoofbeats are real, and I am going to tell everyone.

I do not remember how I got back home when I wake up.

It was nine hours before I heard the horses the second time when I was irritated with my father for reasons I did not understand. I chose to make it the fact that I wasn't allowed to have friends. He was sitting on the couch when I sat on the farthest side away from him with a sour look on my face and my arms crossed. I waited for him to ask what was wrong, which took a long time. They were talking about the country and patriotism on the news, and he was laughing bitterly at the things they were saying.

When he finally noticed me, I told him I was tired of not being allowed to have any friends.

He looked at me as if I were crazy and told me that of course I was allowed to have friends.

I asked him how I was supposed to have friends if I couldn't leave the house.

He told me I could have friends at school.

I told him no one at school wanted to be friends with a girl they could only be friends with at school.

He asked where this was coming from, which is a thing I realized he always does when I might be making a good point.

I told him I was lonely and tired of sitting by myself all the time.

He told me I could always come to him when I am lonely.

I could not explain to him why not.

It was seven years before I heard the sound the second time. We were visiting my grandmother for one of the last times, and it was the last time I would remember, so for me it felt like the last time. This was when she told me about the valley.

She said that there is a valley near the county line, and when people go to it at a certain time of night, they can hear a herd of horses stampeding through the forest, but they checked, and no one has ever kept a herd there. They kept looking because they figured someone was playing a trick on them, and one day, they finally found a horse, only it was pale white with deep black eyes, so they ran because they thought it was satanic, and to this day no one else has heard the horses.

My father laughed bitterly at this, too.

It is one week after I heard the sound for the second time, and I am telling my father about it. I am telling him I have heard the horses grandma was talking about, and he is laughing in response and shaking his head and saying "Oh did you, now?"

This makes me angry in a way I never thought I could get angry at my dad. I tell him he doesn't believe me.

He tells me I must have been dreaming.

I told him I already thought of that, and I wasn't, and it happened twice.

He tells me dreams happen twice all the time. He laughs again, and I hate the sound of his laughter.

I used to think my dad was bitter about many things. Bitter about the government, bitter about his time in the army, bitter about 9/11, bitter about mom, grandma, ghost stories, and God. I am starting to understand that these are all part of the same bitterness.

I think my father is a lemon man. As I grow older, I'm able to peel him back bit by bit, but instead of something sweet inside, there's just sourness. My dad is sour, toe to tip, rind to rind.

It is four weeks after I heard the sound for the second time, and I am in the valley again crying because it feels like the sound is my only friend. The sound is the only thing in my life that does not ask anything of me; it is the only thing that does not want things I do not have to give. I am here because I am angry at my father again. I get angry at dad more and more these days. I don't want him to touch me anymore, I don't want to hear him speak or laugh anymore. I see families on TV laughing and playing with each other, and it feels like they have things I do not. I want what they have. I cannot watch TV without crying anymore.

I ask the valley what is happening to me, but I only hear the silence in response. I did not expect a response, I have never gotten one. I already know that praying for people does not fix them; I am here to hear horses.

The sound comes. I am less afraid this time; I jump up and laugh. I am running with the sound as it passes through me, and I do not trip this time. I am beginning to think I can run as fast as a horse, when a clearing stops me.

The sound is here echoing across the empty sky like thunder with no clouds, but it is not getting farther away this time. It is circling me. The clearing is bathed in soap-foam moonlight, so thick I think I could pass my hands through it and feel it bubbling. There is a horse in front of me. I walk toward it and shout hello. It is pale like a sick person's face, and it is whiter than the moonlight. I shout hello again and it looks at me. Its eyes are black like the darkest parts of the sky, and it begins walking toward me, and suddenly I am terrified.

I am running away now. I can hear it running after me. I am clumsier now, stumbling, falling, and looking back to see it is getting closer, and its eyes are bulging out of its head, and its teeth are moving forward out of its mouth, and its lips are curled farther back than a horse's lips can curl, and its neck is getting longer; its head is moving toward me faster than its body. I scream, I get up, I run again, and I am screaming and running, and the hooves are so loud it feels like horses are stepping on my chest when I am running. I am crying and shouting for my father, but he is not coming.

When I wake up at home, I do not remember how I got away.

It is two weeks before I found the white horse. I am standing in the bathroom because I started bleeding a few minutes ago; I was lying in bed feeling something strange trickle out of me, and when I sat up to rush to the bathroom it felt like I was peeing on myself, so I tried to hold it, but it didn't stop, and when I looked down it was like I had a cup of blood inside me and tipped it over. I have no one to ask what to do, so I stuff a dish towel into my underwear.

I saw on a television show that this means I am a woman now. I look into my reflection and I ask her if she feels like a woman. She does not say anything back because we both know I have never not felt like a woman.

I tell my father to buy me something to catch the blood. He says he will do it tomorrow but I insist he does it today. He asks if I can just hold it and I get angry and say obviously I tried and I can't. He warns me not to take that tone with me. He still waits until tomorrow.

It was late one afternoon when my father called me into his bedroom for the last time. I came in looking angry and impatient, and he asked me why.

I told him we cannot do what he wants to do anymore because I have my period now and I could get pregnant.

He said he was not really my father so it's all right.

He always said he wasn't really my father every time. The first time he said it, it made me cry, because I had done something for him that he said he needed that was painful for me because he was my dad, and I love my dad, and when I cried he told me he was sorry, so sorry, and that of course he was really my dad, of course he was.

So this time I told him no, he really is my dad, and I'm not doing it anymore.

He asked me why I don't like it anymore.

I told him I never liked it, it always hurt.

He got angry and said I should have said something sooner if I didn't like it.

Guilt tapped me on the chest, and I looked down at the floor, and I tried to hold in my feelings, but I cried. I said I'm sorry I didn't say anything sooner. I thought to myself maybe we would be more like a normal family if I had just said no the first time.

I asked him about the war for the first time when I was nine years old.

Why did you have to go to war?

To keep our country safe.

Because of 9/11?
Yes.
Did it work?
No.
Will our country ever be safe again?
No.

The wind is blowing and it's loud in my ears as I step outside of the front door of our house. I am going to the valley for the last time. I walk through the wind and it blows my hair to the side and my skirt to the side, but I don't care; if there's a storm coming, I don't care. I am tired of dreaming of white horses. I am tired of feeling nothing all of the time, and I am tired of running away, and I am tired of being tired; I am turning thirteen in two days.

I walk to the valley and stand in my spot with my fists balled at my sides; the horses sound like fear when they come, but I don't care if I am afraid anymore. I run with them to the clearing; there are angry tears in my eyes. I don't care anymore. Nothing means anything in this world. Wars are fought for no reason, families are ruined for no reason, and when I pray to God about it he doesn't say anything back. Before I heard the horses, all I heard was silence.

I make it to the clearing. It feels larger than the last time, and the white horse is standing in the moonlight grazing. The whole place smells raw and alive, and the sound of the stampede fades into nothing.

When I walk up to him, I can't take my eyes off him. I say hello, and he raises his head and looks at me, and his eyes are still just as black, but it does not look like he wants to eat me. He walks slowly toward me, and I do not run away this time. His hooves click against the ground. He looks down at me and I reach up and touch his neck with my right hand, and it feels warm and fuzzy like a horse should feel, and I reach up with my left hand and pet him on both sides of his neck.

"Hey, you're not so scary, are you?" I say as I wrap my arms around his neck. He lifts his head and picks me up and I giggle like a little girl until he puts me down.

"You're a good horsie, aren't you?" I say, and my voice is light and soft like how people used to talk to me when I was a baby. "Do you have an owner? Someone to ride you?"

When I ask that, he bows his head down to the ground and shows me his back.

I say, "I've never ridden a horse before. I don't even know if I can climb that high."

He keeps his head bowed to the ground.

I look at him for a moment and then I look back in the direction of where our house is. I stare back at it for the longest time before I finally try to climb on the horse, and it's hard, and clumsy, but he is patient, and allows my small clumsy fingers to pull on his hair and squeeze his neck without complaining. Then I am on him, and I feel taller than anyone else in the entire world. I lean forward and wrap my fingers in his mane.

"Are you going to take me away?" I whisper.

He rears back and the stampede begins again. He bolts forward and I don't think I can hang on, but I do, and I am terrified, but then I am starting to smile, and among the hoofbeats I holler "woo hoo!" I feel like if I spread my fingers I could fly away. Then I am laughing, laughing as loud as I can as the herd carries me down through the valley into silence.

Author's note:

This story is based on a rural legend from the "most haunted county in Kentucky," which I've left unnamed here to avoid outing where, exactly, I'm from. The legend goes that there is a valley somewhere near the county line where you can go in the dead of night and hear a herd of horses trampling through, but no one has ever been able to find the herd. Some have reported various things which largely come from a need to attach a perfectly good mystery about ghost horses to Satan. Some say they've seen a pale white horse, or a shack with a pentagram on it, or a goat. I've never personally been able to confirm the existence of any of these things.

SOO-SOO GO BYE BYE

SHELDON BIRNIE

BABY GAL DROPPED HER SOOTHER in a potty full of piss this morning.

My soo-soo, she says, grabbing for it. But I snatch that sucker outta there lickety-split.

Sorry, baby gal, I tell her as the tears start welling in her eyes. Soo-soo go bye-bye now.

Baby gal, she's not really a baby anymore. She's two. Two-and-a-half. Somewhere in there. Probably too old for a soother. But she doesn't go to sleep without one. I figure, this pee-pee-soo-soo situaish provides as good an excuse as ever for baby gal to go cold turkey on that front this evening.

But come seven o'clock, baby gal's screaming blue murder. She won't quit. Now, who's pulling on their boots and parka and warming up the car to drive across town to Walmart to get a new pack of soo-soos instead of kicking back with a couple fancy pops and enjoying the hockey game? Yours truly, yessiree.

Ah what's the harm, my wife figures, bouncing the crying gal on her knee. I don't argue. I hate to hear baby gal cry like that, even though I worry her teeth'll come out all bucked up from sucking a damn pacifier night-in, night-out for years. It'll only take a half hour, right?

Outside, it's cold, been dark for hours. Even though the car's been plugged in since I got back from work, she still has a hard time turning over. This old Nissan's on her last legs, no two ways about it. But an upgrade's just not in the cards. While she's warming up, I scrape the windows. Once they're clear I just sit, tune in the hockey game on the AM dial, and wait on the heater to work its magic.

It was slow going, once the Nissan was rolling. The Walmart's not far, ten maybe fifteen minutes door-to-parking lot. But the roads are the shits, blowing snow whirling every which way. Icy and slick from the bitter cold, the intersections are like skating rinks in these all-seasons. The Jets have been scored on twice since I left the house. The wind rocks my little rust bucket as I cross the bridge over the wide frozen river. If only the wind would pick me up and blow me far away, far to the south where I could cultivate a deeply cancerous tan and never listen to another hockey game on the radio ever again.

I think of my daughter, her rosy cheeks, her tiny fists clenched as she travels through dreamland, soo-soo secure in her jaws. All this to pacify a child.

My phone buzzes in my pocket. I pull it out. My wife, texting new items for me to fetch.

TP
Wipes
Pads
Chips?

OK, I text back, trying to keep my eyes on the road. As I'm passing this line of big-ass houses along the river to my right, each one still all done up with holiday lights, I catch something big and white lumbering along the tree line.

What the shit?

I blink three, four times quick. The window's frosty, streaked with dirt and road salt. But the big white sasquatch-looking motherfucker's still there, moving from the windshield to passenger side window before passing out of sight as I cruise up the road toward Walmart.

Surely, my tired eyes had deceived me. But I never smoke weed anymore, not while baby gal's still up anyway, and I'm only two beers deep here. Whatever I'd seen had probably just been the homeowner, decked out in some faded coverall, covered in snow from head to toe. A giant homeowner, maybe. Andre the Giant sized son of a bitch. Or two teens stacked on top of each other, playing a hilarious joke? Surely not some wayward abominable snowperson ambling through riverfront properties. No fuckin way.

As I pull up to the next set of lights, they turn red. I'm slow on the uptake, thinking about whatever it was I'd just seen, so when I hit the brakes, I'm sliding. Shit bugger damn. Cars are rolling through the green. The Nissan's slowing, but still she ain't stopping. Shit shit shit. I lay on the horn as I pass the stop line, like a slow rock into the house, front end peeling around to the left. Cars creeping through the intersection are blaring their horns back at me as I finally come to rest, well into the first lane of crosswise traffic. A pickup swerves, narrowly missing the passenger side corner of the Nissan. Driver gives me the finger.

Fuck sakes.

Boy, I am rattled when I pull into the Walmart parking lot not five minutes later. I circle the lot, looking for a spot that's not an icy football field away from the front door, and almost crash into the back of a minivan.

Inside Walmart, I nod to the old lady smiling inside the doors in her blue smock against the glare of the bright lights as I pull out my phone and check the wife's texts for the list of what I need to get outta here. Switching the plastic basket from hand-to-hand, the blood slowly thaws in my fingers, and I shuffle along, checking the items off one-by-one.

TP

Wipes

Pads

Chips

Candy bars (for good measure)

The whole time, though, I'm thinking of whatever the hell it was I seen back there in the snow. Some sorta missing link type situaish? Bigfoot? Motherfucking Yeti? For the life of me I cannot figure that shit out. It just don't make sense. I'm standing in line for self-checkout when I realize I forgot the goddamn soothers.

Ain't that just the shits, eh?

Muttering apologies, I snake my way back out of the corral and retrace my steps to the baby section. My girl's really too old for this shit. Aren't we all though, sugar? I grab a couple packs, so as not to have to do this again the next time one rips or goes missing or falls in a plastic bucket full of piss. But this is the end of the line for the soo-soo train, baby gal. For real, this time.

Crossing the parking lot, I'm slow and steady against the assault of the relentless north wind. Safely back at the Nissan, I toss the bag of goods in the passenger seat and crank up the heat. I shut the radio right off when I hear the boys have let yet another in headed into the third. After giving her a minute to warm up, I ease the Nissan out of the lot and back into traffic, slow and steady.

But as I'm getting back close to that stretch of houses up along the bend in the river, I can't sit still. I'm craning my neck, eyes peeled, looking through the frost for that whatever the fuck it was to reappear. Passing the yard where I swear I'd seen the beast lumber through not a half hour earlier, sure enough there's nothing there but trees and snow and darkness, house in back all lit up as though Christmas hadn't been a month ago. No sign of a snowperson, friendly or otherwise.

Shit. I laugh, shake my head, and crank the radio back on, over to an FM rock station. Kick out the jams. Bigfoot ain't real, dummy. Every-fuckin-body knows that.

But as I'm crossing the bridge I'm not convinced. I'm not usually one to buy into that supermarket checkout tabloid wacko-tobacco crap. But what the hell do I know? I work for the telephone company. Maybe there is something to it after all? Perhaps its task is as thankless as mine, and this tall bastard followed the river into town, looking for something to pacify its own squalling progeny out in the icy swamps and barren trees up by the big lake, or wherever the hell it might call home in this frozen world? Whatever it is would probably rather be somewhere warm, wouldn't it? Wouldn't we all?

When I get home, guess who's fast asleep? You guessed it: baby gal. Guess she's been sawing zzzs since about ten minutes after I left the house. About the time I was passing Bigfoot, sasquatch, or whatever out there on the side of the road. Whatever it was that was there and then wasn't.

Mama bear, she's curled up on the couch with a murder show on. I shrug outta my winter gear, flop on the couch beside her for a kiss, crack the bag of chips and settle in. After a couple cold ones, though, I'm still stuck stewing over whatever it was I seen out there. I can't explain it any more than I could a couple hours ago. But I keep glancing out the frosty window to the wind blowing snow between our tightly packed houses, looking for that big old white body to come creeping down the road. Waiting on a furry face to peer back in at us through the glass.

I crack another cold one, dig around for a roach I been saving. If nothing else, I'm sure I know who's been doing the grisly string of murders on this TV show.

Pretty sure, anyhow.

Author's note:

Winter in Winnipeg is cold and dark. The nights are long. When the winds are blowing snow every which way and the temperature rivals that of Mars, folks can get squirrely. What was that figure tromping through the cold, crossing the frozen river at this hour? Surely only desperation or foolishness could drive someone out in this weather, you figure, though perhaps there is another explanation. We don't know everything that goes on in the shadows, after all, do we?

DER BUTZEMAN

EDWARD KARSHNER

THE BODIES DROPPED IN PAIRS. The first was a user and sometimes dealer who delivered for Jimmy's Pizza up on North Court Street. The second was a dealer and leg breaker from Columbus who'd come to the sticks to take advantage of slow-witted hillbillies. He was on a slab, now, missing both his arms and legs. Then, another user with a DoorDash sticker on his Fast and Furious Hyundai died of an overdose. Not two days later, an enforcer from Cleveland turned up dead. Well, his head washed up on the bank of the Kinnikinnick River by Mount Tabor—being deceased, then, heavily implied. *The Kinnikinnick County Bi-Weekly Gazette* (Wednesday and Saturday) called it a "reign of terror."

"I'd hate to be that bloke right now. Eh, mate?" Brodie Morrison said wiping the bar down and looking at Sherriff Jack Brooke, who was taking his supper at the Whistle Pig with his girlfriend, Tess Shiners—who was also Brodie's ex-wife.

Alan leaned back to avoid the towel and then placed his beer back on the bar. He thought of the delicate balance of representing the law in a county that both appreciated you keeping the peace and resented you for doing so at the expense of "sweet but misguided" kinfolk. Either way, it was best to not have bodies pilling up at the coroner's office.

Brodie crossed his arms. He smiled and leaned forward.

"I hear it's a drug war. This county will be on fire. Unfortunate for a new Sherriff, I'd say. You know, to be tested so soon," Brodie said, his smile fading into mock concern.

Alan took a sip of his beer. "I bet you're all tore up over it," he said.

Brodie mocked surprise. "No hard feelings. Seems we all landed on our feet." He tossed the towel over his shoulder and moved to the end of the bar.

Alan finished his beer and looked over at Sherriff Brooke and Tess. They sat at a booth by the pool tables. Jack was twisting a paper straw wrapper around his finger, unrolling it and twisting it back around. Tess was talking, making a point by pushing her index finger into the table. She sat back with her arms crossed. Then, she noticed Alan and waved him over.

He walked over slowly, feeling like he had interrupted their conversation.

"Well, hey, Alan," she said.

"Hey Tess. Sheriff," Alan said.

Jack looked up and nodded.

Tess took a sip of her house red. "You should talk to him, Jack."

There was an awkward pause filled with Tess's side-eye at Jack, who stayed focused on his pint glass of Coke.

"He helped solve a one-hundred-year-old murder. Think what he could do with a fresh one," Tess said.

Jack shook his head.

"Yeah, I'm a folklorist, not a detective," Alan said.

Then, Jack said, "You still living out at the end of Turstin Hollow?"

"Yes. At my great-grandmaw's old place."

"You might be able to help me after all," Jack said.

"How?"

Jack leaned back. "I can't get any of your people to talk to me. Even Uncle Tack couldn't loosen them up."

Alan smiled. "So you need a hillican?"

"That's right," Jack said. "Can you meet me at my office in the morning?"

"Definitely," Alan said.

"And," Tess said, "there we have it. Now will you lighten up a little?"

Jack sat behind his oak desk and sighed. "I need you to understand that this is an ongoing investigation. That whatever we talk about here is strictly confidential."

Alan nodded.

From a folder, Jack took out two sheets of paper and passed them to Alan.

"These are the two overdoses. Both their cellphones last pinged going into Turstin Hollow. My guess? Delivering more than breadsticks and lukewarm Starbucks," Jack said.

Alan read the autopsy reports. "Strychnine?"

Jack leaned forward. "Not overdoses. Somebody knows something. They won't tell me. Might tell you," Jack said.

In the rural areas Alan was from, folks stuck in clusters of families and neighbors. Besides church and festival days, those boundaries were seldom crossed.

Save for the community store.

That was where everyone gathered. Where stories passed for people to tell and for people to hear. If there was anything worth knowing, it would be found at the Sassafras Run General S & T.

The concrete building had been a store, a gas station, a church, before returning to a store once again. The owner, Runt Salisbury, had been running the latest iteration of the store since before Alan and his family moved away. Runt was one of the few people Alan remembered from his first ten years in the hollow.

Inside, the store was a cool, dark respite from the strange October heat. The smell of cardboard, coffee, and bleach pulled Alan back to his childhood, welcoming him home. Runt stood behind the counter working numbers in a large logbook. He looked up when Alan walked in.

"There's Alan," Runt said, closing the book. "I heard you'd come home." He came around the counter shorter and more stooped than Alan remembered. He put his hands on Alan's shoulders and squeezed.

"I bet you need a jimmy cone. Oh, when you was a boy you'd eat 'em till you's sick," he said.

He went to the chest freezer and returned with a generic brand Drumstick.

"Here you go," he said.

Alan smiled as he unwrapped the top. The jimmy cone being better, in his opinion, than its name-brand inspiration based on the use of real vanilla ice cream and the liberal use of fudge.

"How much?" Alan reached for his wallet.

"Oh come on," Runt whistled.

He went back behind the counter.

"You still out at your great-grandmaw's old place?" Runt said.

"I am," Alan said. He took a bite of the jimmy cone and caught the chopped peanuts that fell loose in his hand. He sprinkled them into the waste can by the counter.

"Probably will need to move before winter, though," Alan said.

Runt said, "Probably oughta move before deer season when all them buck Rambos from Columbus come and start shooting at ya while you be taking a piss outside."

Alan acknowledged that Runt made a good point.

"So, you're getting along up there all right, then?" Runt said.

"I like it up there. Sorta getting my mind straight," Alan said.

Runt made a noise in his throat. "Yes, sir. The woods will do that. Especially the woods where your people are planted," he said.

Alan finished his sundae cone and dropped the wrapper in the waste can. He was trying to figure out how to prime the gossip pump.

"Not like that bunch of trash that bought your family's old place. ATV vacations my ass. Your granddaddy woulda chased them off with a stick," Runt said.

Alan leaned his hip against the counter and crossed his arms.

"I haven't had the stomach to go back there," Alan said. "To see what they've done."

Runt scratched his ear. "Ain't what they done. More what they's a-doing," he said.

Alan leaned forward. "Oh yeah?"

Runt nodded, "Hmpf." He pushed himself back against the rack that held cigarettes and rolling papers. He looked askance. "I figure it's all just a drug front. Right there on your land." Runt looked at Alan like he should do something about it. Like it was still, legally, his land.

"Nothing much I can do about it," Alan figured. "Except..."

That got Runt's attention. He leaned forward.

"You think they might be messed up in all this murder business that's going on?" Alan said.

Runt raised a bushy eyebrow so high it nearly wove into his receding hairline.

"I thought you caught stories," Runt said.

Alan said, "I do."

"Sound like a policeman to me," Runt said.

Alan hoped he hadn't blown it. Every episode of The Rockford Files he'd ever seen ran through his head. Then, he decided to be honest. Honest with an eye toward the aspirational.

"Sheriff Brooke asked me if I knew anything about those local boys who died. They were both up this way at the end. I'm just thinking that if that outfit is doing some illegal shit, I can tell the sheriff, the land gets seized, and I can buy it back," Alan said.

Runt turned up his mouth in a sly smile. Then, he looked at his feet and shook his head.

"Well, it's more than just drugs and the usual bullshit," Runt said.

"How so?" Alan said.

"Let's go sit with coffee."

Alan and Runt sat at the metal bistro table situated by the bathroom. They sipped black coffee.

"Now, this is just somewhere between gossip and speculation, mind you," Runt said stirring sugar into his coffee.

Alan agreed with a nod.

"When that bunch over there at your old home place started messing with the land, taking down the barn," he paused and looked at Alan for a reaction, "well, things got a bit irregular up here in the hollow," Runt said.

Alan took a sip of coffee from the Styrofoam cup and waited. He wanted Runt to have his say. To not be led.

"Now, early on, things went missing up there. Tools, building materials. Truth be told, that, sadly, ain't unusual. Seems nowadays, out here, if it ain't nailed down, it'll get took. Hell, back in the day, we didn't even lock our doors. Anyways, those boys from Columbus come in here all pissed off about it. Don't want to call the sheriff. 'What you want me to do?' I say." Runt held out his hands in supplication.

"Then they say to me, 'You ever hear of a butz?'" Runt looked at Alan. "You know what is a Butzemann?"

Alan thought. Der Butzemann. It was an old word—very Dutchy.

He shrugged. "A boogie man? Like a hillican Golem?"

Runt snorted.

"I say to them, 'How you ever hear of such a thing?' The big one, the one with the German cross tattooed on his neck, says to me 'That old woman, Hausland, told me.'" Runt sat back with his arms crossed and winked.

Alan waited before realizing he was meant to respond.

"I don't understand," Alan said.

Runt leaned forward.

"Old Gretchen Hausland? You've never heard of her?" Runt said.

Alan shook his head.

"Well, young man, she is the last of the old-timey yarb workers. Been living alone up there, now, some thirty years. I mean, she's gotta be pushing a hundred now. I figured her dead long ago," Runt said.

Alan did some quick math. Hausland would have been in her twenties while his great-grandmaw was working roots and conjure. He took out his Moleskine notebook and jotted down some notes.

"I figured that whole generation gone," Alan said.

"Me too," Runt said. "That's why I said to that Nazi shit 'You seen Gretchen Hausland? In the flesh?' He gets all testy with me. Says he did. He says she told them that the butz didn't cotton to what they were doing and was making a point of it."

"What are they doing up there?" Alan said.

"Don't know for sure. But, I'll tell you this, if what they's doing brought Granny Hausland down off Orchard Hill, then it ain't good," Runt said.

Alan forgot about the murder mystery. An old-time yarb woman? Still alive now? Well, that was something he couldn't pass on.

"Do you know where on Orchard Hill I can find her?" Alan said.

"For the law or your stories?" Runt said.

"My stories."

"Give me your book there and I'll make a map," Runt said.

Runt sketched out a map on two pages of the notebook. It could have been art.

"Now," Runt said, "you be careful. She's an ornery one. More spirit than woman, at this point, I reckon. So mind yourself."

Alan looked at the map. He said, "This'll get me there?"

Runt sighed. "It'll get you to where you're noticed."

Orchard Hill wasn't really a hill. It was more of a network of interlocking and overlapping hills and hollows creating a fallow buffer between private land and government seizures. As the good road thinned to a series of worn logging switchbacks, Alan kept his Liberty close to the hillside on his left avoiding the sloping section of pitch pine forest on his right. He slammed on his brakes. A beech tree, having come loose from the hillside, lay across the road. He studied the situation through the windshield and sighed. He turned off the Jeep and walked to the tree for a closer look. The tree was old and thick. There was no getting around it.

"Well, shit," Alan muttered.

He looked behind him at the rutted road. He would have to back down to the last elbow turn. There would be enough room there to turn around. He started back toward his Jeep.

"You lost or where you want to be?"

He jumped. The voice behind him out of place, up here, in the silence of the woods.

An old woman stood on the other side of the tree, a safe distance up the road.

Alan had been noticed.

"Gretchen Hausland?" Alan said.

She tilted her head and spit.

"My name is Alan Terrell. I'm..."

"I know who you are. Been waiting on you or one like you," she said. The woman looked at Alan's

Jeep. "Leave it. Ain't nobody coming up this way. Come on."

Alan took his musette bag from the back seat and his Australian stockman's hat from the front. He locked the doors and climbed over the tree. Gretchen Hausland was already around the turn. He had to jog to catch up.

"How'd you know I was coming? Runt tell you?" he said.

She looked at him.

"When you fire on them, someone always comes," she said.

They walked the road side by side until she stopped, pushed him aside gently and started up a narrow deer path. Alan followed her to a clearing. Two wide gardens, separated by a river stone path, led to a roughhewn, square-logged cabin. Next to the cabin sat a rusted contractor trailer, a relic of the construction work from the 1950s.

"We'll sit in the winter house. It's more befitting a conversation such as ours," she said pointing at the cabin.

Inside was a wood stove, a sink with a pump like the one he had in his cinder block hunting cabin. The walls were covered with layers of old newspaper for insulation. She pointed to a chair with a woven wood seat.

"Sit. I'll get us some water," she said working the pump. Clear spring water flowed into an earthenware pitcher.

"I noticed, in your garden, you are growing nicotiana rustica, strong tobacco. That's pretty rare," he said.

"It's a powerful plant. Pure. My seeds are direct lineage from the Shawnee. Their land. Their seeds remain. My work requires power. Not powdered chocolate and rat piss like the smoke we make now," she said.

She put the pitcher and two coffee cups on the butcher's block table.

"Not used to company," she said pouring two cups of water.

Alan quickly removed his hat.

"I'm not used to being company," he said. He looked around for a place to put his hat. On a small work table next to him was a wooden bowl full of dried brown discs. His mouth twisted. Quaker Buttons, from the strychnine tree. Alan looked at his cup of water.

"Runt Salisbury sent me here," Alan said, hoping that would be enough to keep her from poisoning him.

She took a drink of water.

"No. He told you where I was. You's here 'cause you can't help it," she said.

"Can't help what?" Alan balanced his hat on his knee.

"I knew your great-granny Eunice. She was a powerful yarb woman. A good teacher. Knew your granddaddy Bud, too. He was a good man," she said.

Alan felt her watery blue eyes dig into him.

"I know why you are here, too," she said. "You want to know about the Butzemann and them dead men," she said.

Alan took the Moleskine notebook from his back pocket.

"Did you tell the men at the ATV place about the butz? That a Butzemann was taking their stuff? Messing around the construction site?" he said.

She waved her hand.

"That ain't no ATV vacation place. Did you see what they done to your Granddaddy Bud's barn?" she said.

Alan shook his head. "I've been avoiding it," he said.

Granny made a noise in her throat.

"Ain't nobody going to protect the land. See? When there ain't no other way, you need a butz," she said.

"So, you did tell them about the Butzemann?"

"Warned. Ain't none of them going to know otherwise. It's old magic. Nobody does it anymore," she said.

"But you do?"

She adjusted her do-rag.

"How do you make a man? Flesh and bone. Blood and muscle. Breath. Chest and lungs, strong shoulders. But, a man of the earth, of the woods, would be of these things: oak limbs, kudzu, moss and sedge. What lives in there, in the dark hollows and creek banks—the hidden places—lives in him," she said, closing her eyes.

Alan tried to get it all down. She was speaking quickly now.

"But clothes make a man. And a workingman needs working clothes. Long ago, when your granddad passed on, I took some of his clothes. His overalls he wore every day but Sunday, that buffalo plaid shirt that was like a hex to his enemies. His

Wolverine brogans. And a hat. A man needs a hat. He always wore a gray Adam Major. Cocked and ornery. But Adam the first man. The first son of God, the keeper and protector of the land." She paused and took a sip of her water.

If there was a ritual to the Butzemann, he had never read about it. He worked to get it all down.

"A butz isn't just a man. He's a workingman. A poppet of a man who loved the land and would rage against the defilement of the land," she said.

"Is that why you used my granddad's clothes? Because he worked the land?" Alan asked.

"No," she said, leaning forward. "Because he protected the land. In that long-ago time, the government men came for your land. But Bud fought them. Your granddad forgot nothing of his killing time in Europe. But they was many and he was one. So he came to me. Said he needed me to fire on the boss. I did. Sent the Butzemann for that dandy government peacock. That one died. Many more after. Then, the government men backed off. Never came back. I needed one such as Bud again."

"Why? What are the ATV guys doing?" Alan said.

"Poison," she said.

Alan glanced at the bowl of Quaker buttons.

She held up her hand and made a motion like she was braiding.

"I done the same as I did then, now. I made a ragged man. I took that horse hair and I twisted it. Using the name of the man that's on the letters in the mailbox, Mark Buckley. Then, I breathed the smoke onto the poppet, Bud der Nei. The new Bud for a new fight," she sat back.

Alan waited.

"That's how it is. Poison for poison. Violence for violence. Like the Lord says, 'Shall he not render to every man according to his work?'"

"I don't understand," Alan said, closing the notebook.

"But, you know. That's why you come. You must stop the butz before Halloween. Before my spirit leaves him and the Rough Man takes him," she said.

Alan thought. Halloween was three days away.

"Granny, I'm not clear on what you are saying," he said.

She stood up quickly and shuddered. Alan leaned forward and helped her back to her seat.

"It's always easier to be from somewhere than to be there. Because here is where the hard work is." Granny shut her eyes and leaned back.

Alan felt a wave of heat move across his chest.

"In the garten where I made the new Bud, you must bury him. Return him to the soil. The land has called you home, young Alan. It's time you went home," she said.

Alan wrote down "in the garden." He had more questions.

"Now, an old woman needs rest. So I'm going to let you go. Remember, listen to the sounds of the land you're from," she said.

Alan stood up.

"Thank you, Granny. I'll see you soon," he said.

"No, honey you won't, not like this. But I'll be a-watchin' you," she said.

Alan stood up and started his long walk home.

Even though he was staying at the far end of the same hollow, he would go around, taking Corey Road to Eldritch, to come up the back way, avoiding the old home place. Now, he remembered himself home. The land laid as it did in his mind. But, the home place itself, was nearly barren. After the second world war, his grandfather built a cinder block house on the other side of the corn field. When Alan's parents were married, they moved into "Bud's house" and lived there for ten years. But the crown jewel of the old home place was the standard Pennsylvania-style banked barn with a gabled roof. Put up entirely by hand, it was a monument to Bud Terrell's physical and intellectual strength.

The barn was gone, a sheet metal pole barn in its place.

He drove up the dirt road that wasn't the one he held in his mind. It had been widened and laid with gravel. Alan stopped at the fork. To the right, his house sat alone, stripped of the front porch he remembered. A weathered, store-bought sign identified it as the "Office." Alan parked in front of a line of railroad ties placed as parking blocks. With the way the sun played off the dirty windows, he couldn't tell if anyone was inside or not.

Alan switched off the jeep and sat there wondering what to do. He opened the door and stepped out, reaching across the seat for his hat.

The sound of the screen door opening cut the silence and Alan felt it as much as heard it. He looked over the hood of his Jeep. A man in a dirty wifebeater and greasy Dickie work pants leaned against the door jam.

"Can I help you?" he said.

Alan smiled and put on his hat.

"Are you open?" Alan found putting himself at the service of others deescalated most situations. People liked to help people.

The man stroked a sparse mustache.

"No. Lodges won't be open for another month or so," he said.

Alan walked around the front of the Jeep and caught sight of the Iron Cross tattooed on his neck.

"My name is Alan Terrell. I used to live here," he said.

The man pushed himself up and took a step down.

"My granddad built the barn what stood right over there," Alan pointed with a nod.

"It was in the way," he said. "It was a bitch to take down."

Alan smiled. "You must be Mark Buckley."

"What do you want?" Buckley said.

"Just to walk around. I've been gone off for a long time. I wanted to see how things changed and how they stayed the same," Alan said.

Buckley rubbed his shaved head.

"What're you looking for?" Buckley said.

"Nothing. I'm looking for nothing. But it's waiting for me," Alan said.

"What is?" Buckley said.

Alan opened his arms. "This. The land is waiting."

Buckley grinned. He was missing a lower tooth and an upper canine.

"You're one of those hillicans, aren't you?" Buckley said.

"I guess I am," Alan said.

Buckley took the last step down and put his hands in his pockets.

"I've heard a lot about you guys. Still some living way up the end of the road. Haven't seen hardly any of them. I've spoken to one. An old woman," he said.

Alan got the sense he was being looked at like a specimen.

"Some crazy stories, man. Crazy," Buckley said.

"I'd like to hear them sometime. I'm a folklorist. I catch stories," Alan said.

"Thought you might be a cop or something." Buckley said. He itched his nose. "Hey, let me ask you a question."

Alan nodded.

"What the hell is a Butzemann?" Buckley said.

"Like a scarecrow. But it's been enchanted to come alive and protect the land. That's some old folklore," Alan said.

Buckley looked around.

"I think I've seen it," he said, working his hands up and down his pant leg. Alan caught the outline of a pistol in his front pocket.

"I want to show you something," Buckley said.

They walked around the house to where Alan remembered a swing set had been. Empty now, a plastic tarp on the ground alive with the sound of flies and yellow jackets. Buckley pulled back the tarp. Alan stepped backed, pushed by the smell.

"Three nights ago, the rotties we had up there guarding the tool shed got all tore up. Most likely a bear. I guess," he said.

Alan looked at the tangled mass of fur, bones, and meat. He wasn't sure how any of it could ever have been a living animal.

"A bear wouldn't do that," Alan said.

"Yeah. No shit. My partner Paul, he was a sniper in the Marines, set himself up just in the tree line. Going to catch whoever's messing with us," Buckley said.

"What did he see?" Alan said.

"Don't know. Was so bad he just split. Left his gear and everything." Buckley said.

"How long? How long ago did he leave?" Alan said.

"Two days ago." Buckley covered the remains and took a step toward Alan. "So you ask me if you can take a look around? I tell you to fuck right off."

Alan stepped back.

"Tell your hillican buddies, stay away. Leave us alone. Come back again, and there'll be war," Buckley said.

He followed Alan back to the Jeep. Alan was walking. Trying not to run. But aware that Buckley was just as scared as he was.

Just not of the same thing.

Alan opened the driver's side door. "Did it see you?"

Buckley stopped. "What?"

"The Butzemann." Alan shut the door and turned over the engine.

Buckley turned white. "Why? Does that make a difference?"

"A big difference if it saw you," Alan said.

Alan put the Jeep in gear. The woods were full of things real and imagined. He'd leave Mark Buckley to decide which was worse.

Alan wanted a closer look at the old home place without drawing attention. Buckley knew he was poking around. So he'd need another way. There was a seep spring in Eldritch where folks collected medicinal waters. Alan knew that a trail behind it cut over the ridge, a shortcut between hollows that would come out right behind the new pole barn.

So, he waited until hollow gloaming, when the sun started to set early behind the hills, to sneak through the woods that grew smaller in the dying light. The woods seemed unfamiliar now. They contracted up on themselves and shrank from him as he moved in deeper.

Where the woods ended and pasture started, he watched from inside the tree line. Nothing moved but the skeletal golden rod swaying in the wind. He made his way to the pole barn and touched it. The metal was still warm from the day. He listened. There was only the sound of industrial fans blowing along the back. He caught a whiff of something like a jumbo mouse cage, urine. Or, he thought, ammonia.

"Well, shit," he dropped his head. In front of him, along the backside of the pole barn, hidden from the road and what would be the vacation cottages, were piles covered with blue tarps. A late-70s Ford F-150 was parked by the tree line, its bed also covered with a tarp.

He pulled on a pair of leather work gloves and walked quietly to the first pile. The tarp was weighted down with a brick. He kicked the brick off and carefully pulled the tarp back.

Underneath were twenty-some empty propane tanks. He looked closer, careful, though, not to get too close. The fittings on the tanks had tuned blue. Scattered through the tanks were smaller canisters. He rolled one over with his foot, Freon 134a. Alan took out his cell phone and snapped a picture and replaced the tarp.

"Poison," Granny Hausland had said. They were making poison. Alan went to the truck and pulled back the tarp. Large contractor garbage bags filled the bed. He drove a gloved finger into one and pulled it open.

There it was. Among the coffee filters, stained red, were boxes and boxes of Sudafed and generic Pseudoephedrine. Alan pulled the tarp back over the bags and sighed.

He thought about his granddad running the ridge to protect the land from government consolidation. He thought about the old woman living alone in her final years working folk magic to help a man who was no longer alive and a land no one had any interest in protecting. Alan remembered the Butzemann, a protector of a land that could no longer be protected. Alan decided that needed changing.

But the metallic click of a pistol being cocked interrupted his momentum.

"I figured you'd be back. I just thought you'd bring more people," Mark Buckley said. "Are you alone?"

Alan put his hands up and turned slowly.

"Do you think I'd be that stupid?" Alan said.

Buckley wasn't sure.

"Is it you? You the one tearing stuff up? Killed those men the boss sent here? Killed my dogs?" Despite the cool night, Buckley was sweating. His face red. His jaw clenched. "Is it?"

Alan's legs felt rooted into the ground, heavy. He watched the large bore of the pistol barrel move up and down with Buckley's uneven breathing.

"Look, Mark, I just wanted—" He thought. He needed a reason. "My grandfather, when he built the barn that was here," Alan stopped.

Something big was in the woods. Alan could see it just inside the tree line. Not a man nor an animal. It was big on two legs. Its ragged clothes stretched over round muscles that rolled like balls across each other. A smell like rotted potatoes filled the air.

"What the hell is that?" Alan said.

Buckley turned his head stiffly. Stopped and then spun at the sound of it crashing through the trees.

"Damn it." Buckley fired blindly into the woods. "What the fuck is that?"

Alan grabbed the shovel leaning against the Ford and hit Buckley on the back of the head. Buckley dropped to his knees, letting go of the pistol. Alan kicked him hard in the back and Buckley sprawled face down.

"I think you broke my back," Buckley said.

Alan grabbed the pistol and pointed it toward the woods. Whatever it was had moved away. There was quiet and the air returned to the tart smell of ammonia. Alan realized the pistol was empty. The slide locked back.

"You were going to shoot me," Alan said.

From the side of the pole barn, Alan grabbed some rope and hogtied Buckley.

"Jesus, my neck is killing me," Buckley said.

Alan took out his cell phone.

"I'm calling an ambulance," Alan said.

"No, no. Just untie me," Buckley wheezed.

Alan's hands were shaking. Call an ambulance first, he thought. Then, call the sheriff. He looked into the woods. He felt exposed, foolish.

Buckley vomited and his body went stiff.

Then Alan realized he was also too late.

Alan took out his folding knife and pried the "Office" sign off the house and dropped it in the trash barrel by the front door. Jack finished talking to a deputy and walked over.

"It's too early to say. But the ME thinks it was strychnine poisoning," he said.

Over Jack's shoulder, where Mark Buckley had died the day before, men in hazmat suits were slowly dismantling the sheet metal barn. The chemicals from the lab had corroded the inside.

"You didn't kill him, Alan," Jack said. "We found a bag of Quaker Buttons in the lab and some in the kitchen cupboard. Most likely poisoned himself trying to kill the competition."

Alan decided to keep what he suspected about Granny Hausland to himself. After all, what would he say? A yarb woman was yarbing?

Jack turned to watch the bulldozer push over a section of wall.

"That's got to give you some satisfaction," Jack said.

Alan nodded. "It does. Some."

"I noticed your backpack, there. You going for a walk?" Jack said.

"Well, if I'm going to stay here for a while, I thought I'd go out in the woods to do some remembering," Alan said.

"Not a bad idea," Jack said. He started toward the pole barn and stopped. "You did good. No telling how many more would've died."

For Alan, though, there was one thing left to do. Granny had said the Butzemann in the garden needed to be buried before Halloween. It was October 30th. The Butzemann is in the garden, Alan mis-rembered. She said "garten," German for garden but also an enclosure. He had a good idea where he might find Bud the New.

Pulling on his backpack, he headed for the thickest part of the autumn woods, where the path was nearly chocked out by blackberry brambles. The trees wove bare fingers overhead, light streaming down in thin, golden strands. Alan squinted, the sun coming at an odd angle, tossing his perception into a dreamlike obscura.

He cleared the ridge toward The Ladies' Garden. Named because his Great-Grandmaw Eunice was the only one allowed to work it. She grew her herbs and flowers there. It was her place away from the commercial enterprise of men. There, he saw in the clearing on the high part of the ridge, the stone wall, the enclosure.

Alone in the middle of the stone-walled garden, the Butzemann swayed in the wind that chilled the sun's heat. Alan pushed the cross it was on and it gave straight. The doll man stood prouder—the head still sagged. Alan lifted the head gently. He had seen scarecrow poppets in museums and collections that were meant to be representations of Butzemanns, a copy of a copy. But he'd never seen a real Butzemann. Not like this. This was no ordinary scarecrow. This was a Holy Watcher. The protector not just of fields and crops, but the land itself.

"Wie bischt du heit, mein heiliger wachter?" Alan said dropping his backpack on the hard, fallow ground.

New Bud was dressed as Granny had said. The red buffalo plaid flannel was tattered and faded but still held a vibrancy. Alan noticed that the coveralls were stained dark along the front. He touched it. It was hard in some parts. Sticky in others. He took out his bandanna and wiped off his hands. Alan reached around and pulled the head from the upper part of the cross. He carefully took the faded gray fedora from the head and looked inside. "Adam Hats." He remembered the hat from pictures of his Granddad Bud. He put the hat, crown down, on the ground beside him.

The head of the Butzemann was made of a white linen bag filled with what felt like straw. On the face, where the eyes should've been, were Elder Futhark Runes: thurisaz for defense and regeneration and othala for heritage and ancestry. Down the back of the head was a braid of black horse hair. The charm Granny had woven to fire on the men who had desecrated the Terrell home place.

"Well, my goodness," Alan said.

Careful not to tear the shirt any more than it already was, he took the Butzemann from the cross bars and laid it across the ground. He gently wrapped the head and shirt in the coveralls. From his pack, Alan took out a camp shovel and dug. He placed the bundled remains in the hole. He dowsed the contents of the grave with lighter fluid and dropped in a match. Alan watched the flames and smoke take the Butzemann to his place among the honored dead for the Wild Hunt.

"Danki. Bis widder mein dawdy," Alan said.

When the flames had reduced the clothes to ash and scraps, Alan filled the grave with dirt and stones from the wall. He picked up the hat and put it on. Weather and time had tightened the leather band. It was snug against his forehead but he could feel it starting to stretch, to fit.

He started back finding a familiarity in the night like a half dream when you've already been awake. The woods, who had already always been there, welcomed him home without judgment.

Author's note:

In my story "Der Butzemann," I wanted to deal with a supernatural creature other than Bigfoot or Mothman. So, I dipped into Pennsylvania German folklore (my area of SE Appalachia Ohio is very "Dutchy") to look at the Butzemann, a Golem figure who was seen as a magical protector of the land. There was a desperate aspect to the butz in that he was seen as a last chance protector of a threatened land belonging to a threatened people. When all else failed, there was magic. So, I have combined the folklore I grew up hearing in Appalachia Ohio with some good old-fashioned Pennsylvania German folk-magic to tell a story about the psychological effects of displacing a placed people.

Style wise, my writing has been influenced by the work of Manly Wade Wellman. In fact, the Alan Terrell character in this story was originally a modern take on his Silver John character. As the story progressed, I fell under the influence of the great work of H. Byron Ballard and Alan Terrell became more of a "forensic folklorist" for hire. I have also been influenced by the cultural horror fiction of Gabino Iglesias and the Appalachian noir of Ron Rash and Chris Offutt. But, my greatest influence has been the work of David Southwell and his idea of "landscape punk" where conceptual mis-remembering leads to re-enchantment of the individual and the land.

THE TALL MAN
STEVE LAMBERT

FLORIDA, LATE AUGUST, the air outside glutted with ripeness nearly gone to rot, an awful overabundance of spent, rank foliage. But if you're attuned to it, there'll be a day, right at the end of August, where the befouled humidity subsides a little and a faint crispness slides in from the north: the coming of fall.

The day of the boy's arrival was one of these days, and as I walked to my car after work, I inhaled deep of the dry, renewing air, and my spirits were lifted. It's a short commute from the public works office to home, and I drove almost all the way with the windows down, which is a summer rarity.

I noticed Clemons Rutledge, my next-door neighbor, before I noticed the boy. Clemons was long retired and fond of two things: lawn care and other people's business, especially mine. He stood there pretend-watering his lawn, staring off toward my place.

I followed Clemens's eyeline to my front porch and there he sat: a boy of about twenty years old, in cutoff bib overalls, a quart of what looked like malt liquor in a wrinkled brown bag setting next to him.

"See there," said Clemens, a jut of his chin, as I approached. He stuck his thumb over the flow from his hose, creating a thin fan of water. "Got company."

The boy's left leg, I realized as I walked up, was a cream-colored prosthetic. He was thin and olive of skin and sat there, sullen, like an upset child. He took a quick, angsty swig of his malt liquor, glanced over at Clemens, then back to smoldering, hair down around his face like damp moss. It was in this moment that I realized who he was.

"Cousin," I said to Clemens. Whatever Clemens had in mind was, most likely, along the lines of a call to the police or some such punitive humiliation. He liked witnessing and reporting infractions. Nothing criminal, as far as I could tell, had happened here—and this boy, I now realized, was family.

"What's his name then?" he said, walking over to the water spigot on the side of his house, delighted with the prospect of catching me in a lie.

I told him Philip, which also had been my father's name. The young man looked up at me, his mouth approximating a smile.

Clemens frowned and threw down his hose, turned the faucet off.

I pointed at the front door of my house and the young man stood up, steadied himself with his hand on the wall, and got out of my way. I unlocked the door, turned and smiled at him, and he walked in and waited for me to come in and close the door.

I directed him to sit down at my eat-in kitchen table, told him I'd be right back.

I went to my bedroom and put my work things away, changed into comfortable clothes, and came back to the kitchen, opened the fridge, where I found myself a rare English bitter I'd been saving and poured it into an imperial pint glass, one a friend had stolen from a pub for me while he was vacationing in Wales. The pub's name, The Jolly Sportsman, was etched into the glass. I sat down at the table, next to the young man.

"Would you like a glass for your...beer?" I said.

He lifted his quart and took a long sip from it, after which, he burped.

"They's been something happened...Emlyn—I'm sorry about Emlyn," he said.

Emlyn was my mother. It'd been a year since her passing.

"Little late for the funeral," I said.

I moved my chair closer to him and tried looking into his eyes, but it wasn't easy because of all the black hair and his tendency to look at the floor.

"I haven't seen you in, must be, fifteen years," I said. "Almost didn't recognize you."

He gave me a puzzled look.

"Well," I said. "What can I do for you?"

"Do for me," said the young swan.

"Where's Uncle Gregg at these days?"

"Been dead...two months? Not surprised you didn't know. Not many do. That's what I'm here about." After saying this, the boy straightened his posture, folded back his hair and breathed out heavy. He took some time to look around the kitchen.

This news hit me hard, harder than I might have imagined. My father's brother, Greggory, it must be said, had been a philanderer. He was rumored to have illegitimate children all over the southeastern United States and, perhaps, even as far as West Texas. My father and Greggory had been rumrunners in South Florida during prohibition. Their lives, for a time, had been filled with excitement and excess, but my father gave it up once he had earned a nice sum and settled down. Greggory did not. After prohibition, he'd moved over to cocaine. I'd met my uncle once, at a time in my life when most close to me had given up on me and I needed a little help, and he gave it to me, so he was okay by me. But, when I was a young boy, my father rarely spoke of Uncle Gregg, and when he did, he would say deeply black—but unspecific—things about him, things along the lines of, "That man is dead to me."

He just wasn't the subject of much conversation. But this kid, if he was who he said he was, opened up new lines of thought for me. His mother, if I remembered correctly, was Seminole—a beautiful woman named Lilly Perkins. I'd always been intrigued by Gregg and his life. I didn't know enough. Maybe this kid, if he was the real deal, knew some things about my uncle that I did not. Could fill in some gaps for me. He'd have to. God, I thought, my uncle Greggory must have been in his early sixties when this boy was born.

We both sipped our drinks and sighed.

"I'm sorry to hear that, boy. Your daddy meant a lot to me at one time."

"At one time," he repeated. "That one time was a long time ago, wasn't it?"

I sighed out a yep.

"Look," he finally said. "You don't really know me. I don't know nobody from the Moody side." He paused, made a kind of adjustment to his fake leg, pulled his hair back again, revealing black eyes, and continued: "I just know my mama's side, the Perkinses, and they's a bunch of assholes, except momma and Billy. Daddy said the Moodys was no treat neither. But by the time I was old enough to want to know stuff he was so old he wasn't interested in talking—and he wasn't in no shape, really, to go around visiting folks."

He finished his quart of malt liquor and I took the bottle from him and put it in the recycling bin just on the other side of the kitchen door that led to the garage. He reminded me of myself a little at that age—all but the leg, of course. I'd been a bit of a mess when I was a young man, too. No one to blame. I just hadn't the slightest idea how to go about things and not much in the way of adult role models. I sympathized with him. Wanted to help him—the way, if need be, his father had helped me once.

"Why are you here, talking to me?" I said, finally.

"I'm reluctant to say." He paused and glanced doggishly up at me.

"Out with it," I said. "Just spit it out."

"Well, to start with, my daddy ain't died of old age. I'll say that. He was old but it was not natural causes." The boy assumed a fidgety way about him now, quite different from the coolness he'd had up to this point.

I drained my glass.

"He knew them swamps—in and around Big Cypress—better than some of Momma's people."

"I'm sure that's true."

"I was the one who found him. Hadn't seen him in probably a year and a half, which was a typical span of time for us. We was off and on. But I figured I'd go check on the old man. I'd been working up in Wabasso, on the intracoastal. Clamming. Borrowed a buddy's pickup for the weekend." He paused and pulled out a pack of Newports.

"Let's go out back," I said.

We sat down on the picnic table under the water oak in my back yard and the boy lit a cigarette.

"I don't reckon you ever been out to his place— out there in Immokalee. It's not a house. More of a shack. Anyway, he wasn't home when I arrived that Saturday morning, but his fire pit was smoking so I figured he may not have gone far. He got a bluegill hole down the road so I headed there. Didn't have to look no further."

"Let me have one of those Newports," I said.

"These ain't cheap," he said, handed me the pack.

I exhaled and he continued.

"He was face down in the mud. Both his arms was gone, ripped clean off at the shoulder. Both his legs was gone too, the same way. And they was nowhere to be found."

"Goddamn, son. That's grisly." I took a long, icy toke of the Newport.

"Cops figure he bled to death out there. Makes sense. But how did he end up like that in the first place? That's what I want to know."

Why, I wondered, hadn't I heard anything about this? A man found armless and legless in a South Florida swamp is news.

"Don't no one ever report what happens in or around reservations. Dad was nobody, a nobody married to an Indian woman. Less than nobody."

"What do you suppose happened to him?"

"You ever do any hunting?" the boy said.

"Used to bow hunt...deer. I've killed a hog or three. But it's been ten, twelve years."

"Ain't no deer or pig I'm talking about hunting. Ain't no bear or gator, neither. Daddy used to talk about—he ever tell you stories when you was little?"

"Your daddy had some stories. So did mine. Those old boys had lived colorful lives."

"Ain't no goddamn rum-running story I'm talking about. He ever tell you about what he called Halputta-nuntakay: Alligator Man?"

There it was. I had heard a story or two about that.

"I think I know where this is headed, boy. And it's bulllshit."

He kept staring at me.

"I don't think it is bullshit. Wasn't no man ripped his arms and legs off like that."

"Doesn't mean some mythological Florida Bigfoot did it."

"It could—it could mean that." He touched his leg, his fake leg, and sort of adjusted it.

I wanted to know the story behind that leg of his almost as much as I wanted to hear the story behind Uncle Gregg's death.

"Halputta-nuntakay: alligator man..." the boy stopped and smiled. "That's what Dad called it. Said he saw it several times. He knew a little Mikasuki, and enjoyed butchering it, making up his own words. He had a way of improving on things that didn't need improving. Anyway, Chatske—mother—thought it was all bullshit—like you do. Seminole call it Esti Capcaki: Tall Man. All the eyewitness accounts are the same. They all describe it the same way: tall with long, matted hair; slightly stooped stance; quick, smelly; and an eerie howl, like a cross between a bobcat and a lion. Seminole people been talking about this thing for a hundred and fifty years—maybe more. Skunk ape, alligator man, cabbage ape, swampsquatch, whatever you want to call it, man, there must be something to it."

"Your mother was a smart lady. There's no evidence. It's bullshit, no matter what your daddy said."

"Is a smart lady. She's still living. And I don't agree with her. Not anymore."

"So I reckon you're wanting me to go traipse around The Everglades with you, hunting a goddamn swamp monster? That's why you're here?"

"That's right."

"What about that leg of yours? Don't see you being too nimble like that."

"I can get around fine." He knocked his fist against it.

"Were you and your daddy even close?"

"Not the last ten years or so. Just when I was little. But none of that has nothing to do with it. I can't stand the thought of him lying there bleeding to death, helpless. And what if it's real? What if there really is a monster down there?"

The boy looked for a second like he might cry but he gathered himself and looked at me.

"'Sides," he said. "I have a plan. Half a plan, anyways. But I don't really need your help. Just figured you'd want in. Figured if you cared at all about family, you'd do what you could."

Family. Strange, I thought. Hadn't used that word in a long time. This splintered group of individuals never seemed like a family—even when there was more of us. More like a collection of assholes and bitches who hung together out of some strange affinity for each other. Blood magnetism.

We went back inside and I poured myself another beer and poured one for the boy. And I told him to lay it on me. "Let's hear your half-ass plan," I said.

His plan was more like an outline. His mother still lived down there on the reservation. We'd drive down, he proposed, and stay with her. Her brother, Billy, lived nearby and owned an airboat. We'd enlist him and his boat and stalk around that area until we found the fucker and blow him to shit.

"This goddamn thing, if it is real, is elusive as hell. What makes you think we'll find one out there? I imagine if there is one, and it doesn't want to be seen, it won't be seen. Also, wouldn't there be more than one? How would we know we had the right one? Do they speak English? Also, I'm not convinced any of this shit is real."

"We find one, we kill it. Don't really matter if it's the right one or not. Any one is the right one."

"Now I get it. It's more of a revenge thing. Symbolic. You take mine, I take yours."

The boy grinned.

"A gator," I said. "A gator got to him. That's all."

"You know that's not how gators operate. They don't bite off limbs and leave a body. They take a body off under water and hide it under a log or something, let it bloat and soften. Eat it later. Everyone knows that. This wasn't no gator."

"Black bear."

"Black bear down south. Most of their diet is plants and shit. They aren't interested in people. And a black bear would never do to a person what was done to him. Wasn't a bear killed him."

"Have you already talked to your momma and uncle about your intentions?"

"My mother, yes. Not Uncle Billy yet."

I told him I just didn't know if I was interested in heading down south to look for something that didn't exist. Told him it seemed almost pointless to me.

"That's fine. I don't need you. This was a courtesy call. I'm just being polite. But let me ask you—what the fuck else you gonna do? You got a lot of meaningful shit going on in your life at the moment? You got a high-powered career you got to stay on top of? Look, I'm sure you have some paid leave saved up—working for the city the way you do. Take a week, two weeks tops, and do this with me. Tell them it's a family emergency—which is true. Whatever happens, happens."

"What about the police down there in Collier County? What are they doing about all this?"

"Nothing. They've already given up. They're calling it a hunting accident. He wasn't even hunting."

Somehow this kid had my number. And I did feel a strange pull to head down to Collier County, head into the swamp and lurk around. Hadn't been down there in maybe twenty-five years. To be honest—it sounded like a fucking adventure.

"All right. Here's the deal. If I'm in, we pretend this is a regular hunting trip. Everything we do is legal. If we get caught out there by game wardens, we need everything to be set up so that we look like regular hunters out there. It's not deer season yet..."

"Well, it just so happens that it's alligator trapping season—will be till November first. Uncle Billy, I believe, has a permit. That's what I'm counting on. Plus, FWC is more lenient on Indians about this kind of shit. Either way, we'll figure something out. And, yeah, it'll all be above board, like you say. Hell, we will be hunting, right?"

I took a long look at this wild child. What was I about to do?

"Tell you what. I'll do this—on one condition."

He waited.

"Tell me why you have that prosthetic leg."

He looked down at his leg then smiled up at me.

As I said the words, for the first time I realized the strange congruity of the situation: a young man, missing a leg, hunting for a creature that took his father's limbs.

"Well," he said, tapping on it, "wasn't no sasquatch that took it." His eyes lit up.

I guessed, for now, that answer would have to do.

Author's note:

I grew up in Central Florida, in Brevard and Polk counties. I spent many a car-ride, as a child, being ferried back and forth along U.S. Route 192 from Melbourne to Kissimmee and on "Bloody" 520, a state road that goes from Cape Kennedy to the greater Orlando area. Both these roads were largely rural at the time and cut straight through palmetto country: low, creek-veined swamplands. Both roads were saddled with fish camps and mullet joints, but "Bloody" 520 had a little oddity on it called Lone Cabbage Fish Camp, a rickety old shack, as I recall, right along the St. Johns River. You could eat fried fish and hushpuppies here, and you could pay for fairly impressive (and somewhat scary) airboat rides through the St. Johns River and its surrounding wetlands. This was right outside of a town called Cocoa. Inside Lone Cabbage was the disembodied head, in a glass box, of a creature purported to be something called a skunk ape. That skunk ape head seared into my brain. That first encounter, in fact, is so vivid that I can remember asking my dad if the head was real, asking him if there really were Skunk Apes out there in the swamp. I can also remember being vaguely disappointed when he chuckled and said, "No. Of course not. It's a mythological creature. Like Bigfoot." I was also a little incredulous. What did he know, anyway? Hell, I thought, chewing on a nugget of fried gator tail. There might be something out there...

Contributors

SHELDON BIRNIE is a writer from Winnipeg, Manitoba, Canada, who can be found lurking online @badguybirnie.

D.G. BRACEY is from all over, but his origin story began in the swamps and rivers of rural North Carolina. As a young man, he held too many jobs, in too many fields. He calls it research. He has spent the last twenty years as a freelance writer and a teacher. He worked as a columnist and reporter for newspapers and published short stories in various journals. He holds an MFA in Creative Writing from the University of North Carolina-Wilmington, an MA in Writing from Coastal Carolina University, and a BA in Journalism from the University of South Carolina. Currently, he teaches writing classes at Coastal Carolina University and is working on too many projects to talk about.

JON DOYLE is from the UK. His writing has appeared in *Short Fiction*, *Hobart*, *Ploughshares* blog, *HAD*, *The Rumpus*, *3:AM* Magazine and other places.

JAQ EVANS is a speculative fiction author based out of Seattle, Washington. She also leads digital engagement strategy for 350.org. Her work has appeared in *Three-Lobed Burning Eye*, *Fusion Fragment*, and others, and can be found at www.jaqevans.com.

ZAKARIAH JOHNSON plucks banjos and pens thriller, horror, and crime fiction on the banks of the Piscataqua. His recent stories have appeared in *Level Best Books· Best Crime Stories of New England 2021* (crime), *Blind Corner Literary Magazine* (horror), and the Bristol Noir anthology *Savage Minds & Raging Bulls* (thrills!) Following him @Pteratorn (it's a bird) on Twitter and Instagram.

EDWARD KARSHNER was born in Ross County, Ohio, and grew up in the Salt Creek Valley of Southeast Appalachia Ohio, which draws together Ross, Hocking, and Pickaway Counties. He is an Associate Professor of English at Robert Morris University where he researches, teaches, and writes about Appalachian folklore, magic, and mysticism. Karshner enjoys autumn in the Hocking Hills, Chillicothe Paints baseball, and the Circleville Pumpkin Show. He lives in Oberlin, Ohio, with his wife Kim, their children James and Alexandria, and a mixed-breed dog named Carlos. His e-short *The Salt Creek Valley Monkey Dog*, from Mountain Gap Books, is available where all e-books are sold.

STEVE LAMBERT's writing has appeared in *Saw Palm*, *Chiron Review*, *New World Writing*, *New Contrast* (South Africa), *The Pinch*, *Broad River Review*, *Longleaf Review*, *Emrys Journal*, *BULL Fiction*, *Into the Void*, *Cowboy Jamboree*, *Cortland Review*, and many other places. In 2015 he won third place in *Glimmer Train*'s Very Short Fiction contest and in 2018 he won Emrys Journal's Nancy Dew Taylor Poetry Prize. He is the recipient of four Pushcart Prize nominations and was a Rash Award in Fiction finalist. He is the author of the poetry collections *Heat Seekers* (2017) and *The Shamble* (2021), the chapbook *In Eynsham* (2020), and the fiction collection *The Patron Saint of Birds* (2020). His novel, *Philisteens*, came out May 2021. He lives in Northeast Florida, with his wife and daughter, where he teaches part-time at the University of North Florida.

MEAGAN LUCAS is the author of the award-winning novel, *Songbirds and Stray Dogs* (Main Street Rag Press, 2019). Meagan's short work has been published or is forthcoming in journals like The *Santa Fe Writers' Project, Still. The Journal, MonkeyBicycle, BULL, Pithead Chapel*, and others. She is Pushcart-nominated. She lives in Western North Carolina where she teaches Creative Writing and edits *Reckon Review*.

J. S. MCQUEEN is a novelist by day and a short story enthusiast by night. She was born and raised in the deep dark hills of Eastern Kentucky, where she received her undergraduate degree from Eastern

Kentucky University and moved on to a fellowship in the MFA program at McNeese State University. She now teaches composition English and works on her MFA thesis: a novel called *King Maker*, which is about a woman who encapsulates the millennial generation's feelings about being born too late to save their own world, and about grappling with being the heirs to a centuries old crumbling empire, told through the lens of her personal struggles with both the family she was born to and the one she found.

T.A. SIMONELLI is a non-binary writer and the editor in chief for Zines From A Town, a small press in Asheville, NC. They spend their time not writing by making and playing tabletop role-playing games, flitting between different kinds of printmaking and photography like some kind of moth, and doting on their furry children. They are pretty sure that social media is a myth, actually.

Available and Forthcoming from Malarkey Books

Forest of Borders, by Nicholas Grider
*The Life of the Party Is Harder to Find Until You're
the Last One Around*, by Adrian Sobol
What I Thought of Ain't Funny,
edited by Caroljean Gavin
Faith, by Itoro Bassey (January 2022)
Music Is Over!, by Ben Arzate (February 2022)
Toadstones, by Eric Williams (March 2022)
Deliver Thy Pigs, by Joey Hedger (April 2022)
Pontoon, edited by Alan Good (April 2022)
Guess What's Different,
by Susan Triemert (May 2022)
White People on Vacation,
by Alex Miller (June 2022)
Your Favorite Poet, by Leigh Chadwick (July 2022)
Man in a Cage, by Patrick Nevins (August 2022)
Fearless, by Benjamin Warner (September 2022)
Don Bronco's (Working Title) Shell,
by Donald Ryan (October 2022)
Thunder from a Clear Blue Sky,
by Justin Bryant (November 2022)
Un-ruined, by Roger Vaillancourt (December 2022)

malarkeybooks.com